PUFFIN BOOKS

ERASED

The so-called normal world had never existed.
It had been a skin, a thin covering over a world
horribly more complex and frightening
than he could have imagined.

GW00726714

Nick Gifford also writes adult novels under the name Keith Brooke. As well as writing, Nick develops websites and lives with his wife and children in north-east Essex.

www.nickgifford.co.uk

Books by Nick Gifford

ERASED

FLESH AND BLOOD

INCUBUS

PIGGIES

NICK GIFFORD

ERASED

PUFFIN

PUFFIN BOOKS

Published by the Penguin Group
Penguin Books Ltd, 80 Strand, London WC2R ORL, England
Penguin Group (USA) Inc., 375 Hudson Street, New York, New York 10014, USA
Penguin Group (Canada), 90 Eglinton Avenue East, Suite 700, Toronto, Ontario, Canada M4P 2Y3
(a division of Pearson Penguin Canada Inc.)
Penguin Ireland, 25 St Stephen's Green, Dublin 2, Ireland (a division of Penguin Books Ltd)
Penguin Group (Australia), 250 Camberwell Road, Camberwell, Victoria 3124, Australia
(a division of Pearson Australia Group Pty Ltd)
Penguin Books India Pvt Ltd, 11 Community Centre, Panchsheel Park, New Delhi 110 017, India
Penguin Group (NZ), cnr Airborne and Rosedale Roads, Albany, Auckland 1310, New Zealand
(a division of Pearson New Zealand Ltd)
Penguin Books (South Africa) (Pty) Ltd, 24 Sturdee Avenue, Rosebank, Johannesburg 2196, South Africa

Penguin Books Ltd, Registered Offices: 80 Strand, London WC2R ORL, England

www.penguin.com

First published 2006
1

Copyright © Nick Gifford, 2006
All rights reserved

The moral right of the author has been asserted

Typeset in Bembo by Palimpsest Book Production Limited, Polmont, Stirlingshire
Made and printed in England by Clays Ltd, St Ives plc

British Library Cataloguing in Publication Data
A CIP catalogue record for this book is available from the British Library

ISBN-13: 978-0-14131-732-8
ISBN-10: 0-141-31732-9

Contents

I

Another Normal Day

It was just another normal day, much like any other. Liam Connor didn't know it would be the last normal day of his life.

Liam was fifteen. He was a bright boy, never top in his class at anything, but always up there. He fitted in. He had lots of friends. He had parents he admired, and he split his time between boarding school and living with his mother and father in their comfortable town house on the outskirts of Norwich. His life could hardly have been more settled.

Liam Connor had been living a lie. Only . . . it turned out that it was a lie no one had thought to let him in on.

Liam Connor was about to find this out.

Liam jumped out of the train as soon as the door would open. It was a Friday evening in the middle of May and normally he would be at school over the weekend. Today, though, they'd granted him an exeat, special permission to leave early and head for home. His father was back from his travels, and Liam and his parents were going to spend the weekend together.

Liam left the station with his bag over his shoulder and crossed on to Riverside Road. A few minutes later he was on New Chapel Road, which cut across one corner of the Heath. Almost home.

He was hot from the walk and from carrying his weekend bag in the May sunshine. It was only a couple of weeks since he'd last been home, but then it had just been him and Mum. His father worked for the government and travelled a lot. Ministry of Defence, Liam thought, although he wasn't sure. One time when he'd asked, his dad had just given one of his winning smiles and shaken his head. 'Sorry, Liam. I can't tell you what I do. Top secret. If I told you I'd have to kill you . . .' Liam liked to think that was true, but he suspected his father did something altogether unglamorous: more carpet fitter or catering consultant than 007.

Liam paused and let his bag slide from his shoulder, catching the strap in one hand as it slithered down his arm. He rolled his shoulders, wondering why he'd packed so much just for a weekend.

The house looked just the same as it always did. Detached, set back from the road, slightly shielded from view by three silvery eucalyptus trees. There was no sign of anybody at home, no car in the drive. It was probably in the garage, he thought, although Mum hardly ever bothered to park it in there.

He crunched a diagonal route across the drive, then crossed the small patch of front lawn.

The front door was open a short way, as if it had been left for him, or as if someone had casually forgotten to close it upon leaving. He pushed on it gently and it was at that moment that he started to understand that something was very seriously wrong.

He paused on the doorstep. A blackbird clacked angrily from the fence. A car went slowly past, classical music playing softly on the stereo. Somewhere, he heard the whine of a distant lawnmower.

Despite all the normal sounds and smells, despite the fact that nothing was obviously amiss, his heart raced and sweat broke out across his brow.

He dropped his bag and went inside.

The hall was no different to usual. Polished floorboards, dark wood panelling covering the lower half of the walls, stairs off to the left turning at right angles after five steps. A tall mirror was on the wall in front of him. His short blond hair stood in haphazard tufts and spikes, and automatically he reached up to smooth it. He could see the apprehension in his own eyes.

'Hello?' His voice sounded strong. It didn't betray the tension he felt. They taught you to project your voice at school.

He turned to the right and pushed at the living-room door.

Inside, it was as if a whirlwind had struck.

He went in.

The sofa had been tipped over on to its back and Liam could see that the fabric panel stretched across its base frame had been slashed, as if someone had been searching for something. The armchair was on its side, slit open too. The antique, glass-panelled bookcase had been tipped forward and broken glass was scattered over the floor around it. The Lucien Freud print of a greyhound had been ripped out and its frame shattered. Family photographs and books had snowstormed across the floor. A wooden-backed chair that had once stood against the wall by the bay window had been smashed into the widescreen TV and now stuck out into the room like some weird kind of sculpture.

Liam stood very still.

Now he regretted having called out. What if they were still here? Whoever 'they' were . . .

He couldn't hear anything from within the house, only the distant sounds of normal life outside.

Mum . . . Dad . . . where were they? Was this the aftermath of some kind of row between them? But his parents never fought. Had they been here when this happened . . .?

He went through to the dining room and it was in a similar state: the Welsh dresser tipped forward across the table, smashed crockery spread over the table and floor.

He hoped his parents hadn't been here. He didn't want to find them . . . broken.

In the kitchen, all the cupboards were open, their contents emptied on to the floor. Out in the garden, nothing seemed to have been touched.

He went to the stairs and hesitated. Should he make a lot of noise, or go up silently? Or should he just leave?

He went up, treading carefully.

He stood on the landing and eyed the half-open doors: his parents' room, his room, the spare, the bathroom. Everything remained silent.

He nudged the first door open with the toe of his

school shoe. There was more upheaval in his parents' room, but it looked less violent here. Clothes had been dragged out of the wardrobes and drawers, but nothing had been smashed. Liam could almost kid himself that this was just the normal mess of busy lives.

In the spare room, boxes had been ripped open and the papers from his parents' desks were everywhere. Their computers were on the floor, cases ripped off, gutted. The bathroom seemed largely untouched.

He hesitated again before the door of his own bedroom, then went in.

Suddenly it was just a normal day again. Back home for the weekend. His bed, his World Cup football chart, the crystal radio set he had built at Christmas, his science-fiction books. The window was open on the first catch: his mother must have been airing the room ahead of his return.

He shut the door and sat on the bed, pulling his knees up to his chest, suddenly shaking quite uncontrollably. He jammed his eyes tightly shut and tensed his whole body, struggling to control the tremors. He felt sick and he felt scared.

What had happened here? Where were Mum and Dad?

They knew he was coming home on the early evening train. Why weren't they waiting for him? Why wasn't Dad in the kitchen cooking one of the huge feasts he liked to prepare, and Mum in the living room, righting the furniture and clearing up the mess?

It must have been kids. Vandals. Or burglars, stealing anything they could carry and then trashing the place just for the hell of it.

He took his phone out of his trouser pocket and flipped it open. No missed calls, no unread texts. He called Dad's mobile but only got through to the answering service. The same with Mum's.

He tried another number. On the fourth ring it was answered. 'Yes?' said a familiar voice. 'What is it?'

'Kath,' said Liam. 'It's me. Little brother.'

'Oh, hi. How's things, littl'un?'

'I . . . Do you know where Mum and Dad are?'

'No, why should I?' Kath hardly ever spoke to their parents, even though she only lived a couple of miles away across the city. 'Where are you, Liam? You okay?'

'I'm home. I came back for the weekend. They're not here. I don't know where they are.'

'Probably out shopping or something. You sure they were expecting you? It's not half-term yet, is it?'

'They invited me back, Kath. Listen . . . the house . . . the place has been trashed. Something terrible has happened here. I don't know what to do.'

There was a silence then. Eventually, Liam broke it. 'Are you still there, Kath?'

'I'm here, littl'un.' Her voice had changed, the tone suddenly flat and tired. 'Are you okay, Liam? Have you spoken to anyone? Have you called the police?'

'I've only just got here,' he said. 'No one's here. I tried Mum and Dad's mobiles but they didn't answer.'

'Okay. Listen to me. You need to get yourself out of there. Come away right now – over here to my place. Once you're here we can work out what to do. Do you understand?'

Liam was only too glad to hear this. All of a sudden

the thing he wanted most in the world was to get out of this place.

Just then, the front door banged open against the doorstop, a familiar sound to Liam.

'Hey, Kath,' he said, rising from the bed. 'I heard the door. It's probably Mum and Dad. I'll call you back.' He ended the call and slipped his phone back in his pocket.

Easing his bedroom door open, he stepped softly out on to the landing.

It was silent downstairs. Maybe it had just been a breeze catching the door, swinging it open against the doorstop.

Then there was another sound, a muttered word. It was a man's voice, too soft for Liam to be sure but it could easily be his father.

He peered down the stairwell. He saw the top of a man's head. Dark hair cut short. Balding on the crown. No, not his father. Liam could see a corner of the hall mirror from here, and what he could see of the man's face confirmed this. The man's features were too sharp, his face too thin. His dark eyes flicked about, giving him the air of a twitchy animal.

Liam kept his head down. If he could get back to his room, he could climb out of the window, lower himself and then drop to the back lawn.

Just then, deep in his trouser pocket, his phone rang. The man looked up and saw Liam. His mouth opened, but no sound escaped. He reached for the banister and stepped on to the stairs.

Liam backed away, but the man came up quickly. He was tall, wearing a shabby grey suit and a dark tie, loose at the neck. He had the kind of dark, peppered stubble that could never be shaved away. 'I don't think you're going to answer that, are you?' he said in a London accent.

Liam reached for his pocket, but didn't take out the phone.

He glanced towards his bedroom door, but realized his chance of escaping through the window had gone. He eyed the gap between the man and the top of the stairs, wondering if he could barge past.

'Don't even think about it,' said the man. 'Even if you get past me there's a constable on the door.'

Constable . . . 'You're police?' said Liam, relief flooding in. The phone kept repeating its tune.

'What did you think I was?'

'I . . . Something's happened,' said Liam. 'Downstairs. Up here too.' The phone stopped. A second later, it started up again.

'Looks like we caught you red-handed, doesn't it?' said the man.

It took a moment for Liam to work out what he was implying. 'What do you mean? It wasn't . . . I *live* here. I've just got here and found it like this.' The phone stopped after three rings this time and remained silent.

'Why should I believe that?'

'Downstairs,' said Liam. 'I can prove it.'

The man stepped aside. There are some people you just dislike immediately and this was one of them. The lopsided smirk on his face, the twitchy movements of his eyes, the way he seemed to make accusations with everything he said. 'You first,' he replied, waving a hand towards the stairs.

Liam stepped past him and headed down. Through the open front door he could see the back of a man in police uniform and it was only then that he realized he had seen no proof that this man following him down the stairs actually was a policeman, as he claimed. The sight of the uniform reassured him.

In the front room, Liam stooped to retrieve one of the photographs from the floor. It was one his mother had taken: Liam and his father at Christmas. The two of them: blond, grey eyes, the same rounded features. He handed it to the man, who squinted at it and then stared at Liam. He shrugged. 'Looks like you,' he said. 'You know how it seemed.' That appeared to be it, as far as apologies went. 'This your dad? Where is he? Where are your parents?'

'I don't know,' said Liam. 'They should have been here.'

'So who did all this, then?'

'How should I know?' Liam's head was hurting now, a deep throbbing ache behind the eyes. 'I don't know what's going on.'

'Is anything missing?'

Liam shrugged. Only his parents.

'So what do they do? Your parents.' As he spoke, the policeman walked slowly round the room, poking at the debris with his feet, occasionally squatting to pick something up for a closer look.

'Mum works in a research centre at the university. Medical research. Dad . . .' He stopped, flashing back to how his father always avoided the question of exactly what he did for a living – something that involved a lot of travel, a lot of meetings in London, a lot of secrecy.

9

'Yes?'

'He works for a government department. Civil Service. He's away a lot.'

'Why would anyone want to do this?'

Liam shrugged again. 'They're missing,' he said. 'My parents. They should be here but they've disappeared. What are you going to do?' He rubbed at his aching head.

'We'll do what we can. Has anything like this happened before?'

Liam shook his head. Everything had been pretty much perfect before. A comfortable life, an easy existence. Oddly, he realized that the sun seemed to shine from a blue sky in all of his childhood memories. Life really had been good.

But now . . . Now his head hurt.

'My sister,' he said. 'I need to get to my sister.'

They drove him there in an unmarked car. A uniformed man was at the wheel and the twitchy plain-clothes man sat sideways in the passenger seat so he could stare back at Liam. Down to the inner ring road, past the blocky grey Catholic cathedral and then out on Unthank Road.

Kath had a first-floor flat in a terraced street here, in the heart of student bedsit land. Liam watched from the car as she answered the door to the policeman, her face pale. They spoke for a few minutes, then the man gestured and the uniformed driver came round to let Liam out.

'Hey, littl'un,' she said. Liam was a few centimetres taller than his sister, even though she was ten years older. They stood awkwardly. Kath never had been one for shows of affection. She had her mid-brown hair tied back from her face, and it looked to Liam as if she had put on a few kilos since he'd seen her at Easter.

'It's okay now,' she said to the policeman. 'We're okay now. You can go.'

She ushered Liam in and shut the door, leaning back on it.

'What's going on?' he asked, but she just waved at him to go up the stairs to the flat.

'It's Kath. Liam's with me at the flat. Call us. Let us know what's going on.'

His sister sat back, replacing the telephone on its rest. She'd left the same message on both their parents' mobile phone answering services. Liam had texted them both too. 'Email,' he said now. 'We should email them, in case they check that.'

'We can do that in a minute,' said Kath. 'We'll have to go out to an Internet cafe. I'm not online here.' Kath was a nursery nurse, which she always used as her reason for the things she couldn't afford, like computers and a car. 'So tell me again, Liam: why did you come back this weekend in the middle of term? Was there anything odd about the invitation?'

'Well actually,' said Liam, 'I suppose there *was* something a little odd about the invitation. It was meant to be a surprise.'

2

RSVP

On the day before Liam's return home, it had looked like being an unusual weekend for altogether different reasons. He had been going to join the Elites.

When Liam was not living his perfectly normal and comfortable lie of an existence with his parents in Norwich, he boarded at the National Academy for the Talented and Special, out on the Suffolk coast near Wolsey.

Despite its rather grand name, NATS was a fairly ordinary boarding school much like many other such schools scattered around the country. Its main function was to provide schooling for the children of men and women in the armed forces and diplomatic services: while the parents moved around the world with their work, their children stayed at NATS, giving them some form of continuity. NATS wasn't only for forces children, though, and there were pupils from all kinds of backgrounds, many of them on coaching scholarships because of their special abilities and talents.

The NATS joke was that it was a school for Talents and Grunts – the scholarship kids and the forces kids. Liam was a Grunt: there because his father must have pulled strings to get him in. He spent most of his time with the Talents, though, because apart from anything else they just seemed more fun.

'Hey, Grunt, pour the tea, would you? There's a good chap.'

'Pour it yourself, you lazy arse,' said Liam, balling up an old sock and throwing it across the room at Anders, who was lying back on his bed, an open book resting across his face, just a sweep of black hair visible above the cover. Anders was tall and rake-like. Stretched out, he was almost too long for his bed. It was Thursday afternoon, in the hour between end of lessons and dinner.

Liam yawned. He had work to do, but he couldn't be bothered. He swung his legs off his bed and sat up. He shared this narrow room with Anders Linley in Sherborne House, which was not really a house at all, but the east wing of the main NATS hall of residence. Anders was a pain, but a good-natured pain. Liam poured his room-mate a cup of herbal tea from the pot and put it on his bedside cabinet.

'One lump of arsenic or two?' he asked.

'Oh, whatever.'

Liam sat at his desk and peered into his hamster cage. Skiver was fast asleep in a nest of shredded paper.

There was a knock and the door swung open. The acne-pocked face of Wallace, the corridor prefect, loomed round the door. 'Hey, Connor. You're wanted. Principal Willoughby.'

Principal Willoughby was an elderly and genial man who had once been Somebody in the diplomatic service before taking charge of NATS. Liam headed down to the ground floor, and a short time later he knocked on the principal's door.

'Ah, Connor,' said Willoughby as Liam entered the room. 'Come in, come in.' Principal Willoughby was seated behind a deep desk with a leather surface. He was a thin man, with white hair and a long, hooked nose. Behind him, tall leaded windows gave a view over the sports fields to a band of pines and evergreen oaks stretched along the horizon.

'Sir?' Liam stood politely, his hands behind his back.

The principal indicated a flat computer screen with a raised index finger. 'I've been looking at your results,' he said. 'A very interesting set.'

'Results, sir?'

'Your tests. You know we monitor our students' progress very closely. We need to thin out those who aren't suited to the NATS regime and direct them elsewhere. And also, we need to identify and nurture those with talents. We *are* here for the talented and special, after all.'

'Sir.' Liam wondered what he was leading up to. As far as he knew, he excelled at nothing in particular. That was the downside of studying at a school like NATS: surrounded by geniuses of one form or another, it made people like Liam feel very ordinary indeed.

'And you wonder what your talent is, don't you?'

Liam nodded. For a moment it was as if the principal had read his thoughts.

'Sometimes the more interesting talents can be late to emerge,' said Willoughby. 'But here at NATS we are very good at finding them. Your talent? Who knows. Maybe you're merely a clever but fairly ordinary young man, which would be no bad thing at all. But I think we need to encourage any talents to emerge if they are there. Who knows? You might have what it takes to be fast-tracked into Senior House. I've spoken to your mother about this. She is very positive. Have you ever considered the Elite Forces Cadets?'

Liam was thrown by the question. He was still startled at the suggestion that he might be fast-tracked, and more, that they'd taken the possibility seriously enough to tell his parents. Senior House was a wing of the school which stood slightly apart from the rest of NATS. It was a separate building for a start, unlike the other Houses which were really just divisions of the main building. Most students didn't get to Senior House: while the main school was for the Talents and the Grunts, Senior House was for the Special.

'Cadets, sir?'

Most schools like NATS had a combined cadets force: a military club for teenagers who might go on to join the real forces. Given NATS' nature as a school at least partly for those from military families, the cadet forces here were a popular activity. The so-called Elites, though . . . While the combined force went on weekend exercises and learned survival skills, signalling and sailing, about the most active thing the Elites did was conservation work over on Wolsey Point. It was another Grunts and Talents division.

'You should join in with things like the Elites, Connor. The activities help refine your talents. You may see it as a frivolous pastime, but believe me, there is nothing at this school that is not carefully thought through. Everything works towards the assessment and maximization of each individual's abilities. Even this conversation. You are being offered an opportunity. Your response will be noted, added to your record. Everything informs our judgement of the person you are, Connor.'

'Sir.' All this seemed to make sense to Liam. It was good that NATS paid them such close attention.

'This weekend there is an Elite Cadet Force meeting – Saturday morning at nine in the Junior Common Room. I hope to see you there.'

'Thank you, sir.'

'You should come along.'

Hayley was in the Elites, so she *would* say that. Short and stocky, with blonde hair to her shoulders, she sat back on her elbows, face tipped up to catch the evening sun. 'It's an interesting crowd: people like us, a few Grunts. I don't know, there's a different buzz. You know?'

'She's right, Liam, in her sweet but clumsy way.'

Hayley glowered up at Anders, who sat on a horizontal bough of Three Trunker, his long legs dangling idly. This place had become something of an institution for the three of them: out beyond the sports fields, where the ground became sandy and the pine trees grew up from the gorse. Three Trunker was an ancient Scots pine whose trunk split three ways at ground level. You could climb Three Trunker and see right across the creek to Wolsey Point and the ruins of the old military base there. Three Trunker was their place.

Liam should have known the two of them would gang up on him if he mentioned his chat with old Willoughby. Now, his room-mate was looking quite intently at him from his perch up the tree.

'Haven't you noticed?' asked Anders. 'Some of us — there's a spark. A glint of something different. Something exciting. And some are just . . . flat.'

'You mean Talents and Grunts,' said Liam.

'Sort of,' said Anders, 'but more so. There are people who will go on and make a difference in the world, and then there are all the rest. Which group do you see yourself in, Liam? Old boy Willoughby thinks he sees something in you. They test us thoroughly enough, so they should be able to see, I suppose.'

'Why the Elites?'

'It's just one of the things they do with us. One of the ways they filter us out. They identified me as soon as I came here, of course. But I always thought you might be one of the ones with a spark, Connor. Just a slow developer.'

'I think that's Anders' sweet way of paying you a compliment,' said Hayley.

'What sort of things do you do in the Elites?'

Hayley looked away.

'Top secret,' said Anders lightly. 'Not allowed to tell.'

'So when have you ever done what you're told?'

'We do lots of stuff,' said Hayley. 'A lot of the time it's just like a club, a good crowd. There are computer games, which I think are a kind of way of developing your mental powers. Conservation work on the Point, and teamwork games. Sometimes . . . it's all just a blur and you forget half of what's gone on.'

'Are you going to come along, then?' asked Anders.

It all sounded a bit creepy to Liam, but he trusted Anders and Hayley. He felt a warm wave of encouragement and support from them, as he had from Willoughby. He could try it, at least, he supposed. 'Okay,' he said. 'You've convinced me. I'll come along. Saturday, yes?'

Walking back on the sandy trail towards the school, Liam suddenly felt uplifted. It was a glorious May evening, the sun still warm, bees buzzing over the blazing gold gorse, crickets cheeping from the long grass. He felt as if he was making progress. There was nothing at all bad in his life, but now this was something extra, something good. It was easy to forget how closely life at NATS was monitored and controlled, but to know that those doing so thought he was worth special treatment and encouragement was very exciting, even if it did only mean that he was going to have to spend his Saturdays stuck in the Junior Common Room with the Elites when he could be out playing cricket or tennis instead.

His phone bleeped from his pocket to tell him he had a message.

He took it out – the text message was from Dad. 'Home 4 the wknd? Surprise 4 mum. CU fri. Rsvp.'

'Oh well, maybe next time,' Liam told his two friends. 'Looks like I've got a ticket out of here for the weekend. Dad's home.'

'Jammy swine,' said Anders. 'How did you swing that?'

Anders' parents were in the Middle East. No term-time breaks at home for him.

'You should come next time, though,' said Hayley. 'You'd like it.'

Principal Willoughby was fine about it when Liam asked for permission to go home for the weekend. 'I spoke to Linley and Warren about Elites,' Liam said. 'I was going to come along.'

Willoughby nodded. 'Of course you were,' he said. 'It was the correct choice. You'll come next time instead.'

When Liam left Willoughby's office, he called up his father's message again and thumbed a reply: 'I'll be there. Usual train fri. CU.'

Liam spent most of Friday's lessons distracted. Realization that he had been singled out – even as a slow developer, to use Anders' term – was more of a shock to him than he had first realized. He kept catching himself having completely lost track of what the teacher was saying, staring about at his fellow pupils instead. Who was special and who was not? Who were the ones with the spark?

He emerged from the grand front door of the main building at four, his weekend bag slung over his shoulder. NATS had once been some kind of stately home. It was built from red brick with stone lintels and a wide sweep of stairs leading down from the pillared entrance. In the Second World War it had been a military hospital, and then some time after that the first of the extra wings had been added at the back and it had become a school. From the front, it still looked like somewhere the National Trust should be running – more cream teas than baked beans.

The long drive stretched out ahead of Liam, a half-mile walk to the small road where the number 84 bus passed by every two hours. Tall poplars lined the drive. The grounds on either side, once landscaped and maintained by a team of gardeners, had long since been rented out to local farmers, and now were thick with rows of sugar beet.

Partway along, Liam heard the sputtering of a motor-bike, and he turned to see Jake approaching. Jake worked in the kitchen. He had the kind of wild good looks and confident manner that meant half the boys wanted to be just like him and half the girls fancied him. He was prob-ably only about nineteen, but that and the fact that he worked here put him on the other side of the adulthood divide. It was a shock to think that Jake was far closer in age to Liam than to the teachers.

Rather than roaring past, as Liam had expected, Jake slowed, then stopped, a long leg stretched out to steady him. He flipped up his helmet's visor and said, 'Hi. Liam, innit?'

Liam nodded. Jake liked to mix with the older kids, but had hardly ever spoken to Liam.

Jake nodded at Liam's bag. 'Going for the bus? Where you heading? I'm off to Wolsey if you fancy a ride.'

'Thanks,' said Liam, 'but I don't have a helmet . . .'

Jake shrugged. 'Only matters if you crash or if the cops see you, dunnit? We'll go along the bridleway if you're worried.'

Out of the corner of his eye, Liam saw the bus winding

its way along the lane. He could still make it if he hurried. 'Thanks,' he said again.

He glanced back towards the school. No one appeared to be looking. He swung a leg over and put his feet on the rests that Jake pointed out. 'Hang on,' called Jake, and they were off.

At first Liam was terrified at the speed, and at the mad way they seemed to bounce about with each imperfection in the drive's surface. He fumbled, but couldn't find anything to hang on to – no convenient handles on Jake's leather jacket. 'Behind you,' Jake called, and cautiously Liam reached behind and found a metal grab rail.

They roared down the drive and then swung out into the road. Jake seemed to have forgotten about the bridleway, much to Liam's relief. The ride was rough enough even on a normal road.

And then . . . he became aware that he was enjoying it. The air blasted across his face, taking his short hair by the roots and tugging it back. The roar of air across his ears drowned everything out, and he realized with relief that he wouldn't have to make small talk with Jake, the so-cool kitchen porter who wowed the girls and played bass in a punk band and smoked hand-rolled cigarettes in the yard behind the refectory.

They rushed through the narrow Suffolk lanes and across the bridge at the top of the creek. Then they were heading back down again on the other side of the water, or rather the mud, as the tide was well out now.

'Where to?'

They were in Wolsey now – only a few minutes on the

bike, when it was twenty on the convoluted route used by the bus.

'The train,' called Liam, turning away from the disapproving looks of an old couple on the pavement. He was still in NATS uniform . . . What if he was reported?

It was a small station, the end of a tiny rural line that forked off the main London to Norwich line. Jake pulled up at the space marked out for taxis and put his feet down for balance. 'Okay?' he said.

Liam scrambled off the back of the bike and nodded. 'Thanks,' he said, struggling for words once again. 'Thanks.'

With a roar, Jake was off. Liam turned towards the little station building, reaching for his wallet. A whole weekend at home with Mum and Dad. It was going to be good. He just knew it. He felt it in his bones.

3

Emerging from the Dark

The naked mole rat spends its entire life underground, living in a colony, tunnelling through the earth in search of nutritious roots and other titbits. Forever in darkness, the mole rat's world consists only of soil and roots, of other mole rats and worms and other underground creatures. It is entirely unaware of the outside world.

There is a completely different world beyond the darkness.

Night-time and still no word. Liam lay curled awkwardly on a sofa that was too short for him to stretch out, in a borrowed sleeping bag that smelled of dusty cupboards. He had been woken by drunken shouting coming from the flat downstairs. All was quiet now, but he was stiff and sore from lying uncomfortably. A street light burned amber through a thin curtain, casting the room in the kind of half-light that both obscured the details and yet lit up enough to hint at all those things you couldn't quite see. Somewhere, a baby cried.

He and Kath had spent a desultory evening, two people who realized that they didn't know each other anywhere near as well as they should. One of the few things they had in common was that Kath too had been to NATS. But even there they differed. Kath had only lasted a term or two before returning to a state school in Norwich, while Liam, now, was being fast-tracked. Even the Grunts had to make the grade.

They hadn't talked about NATS that evening. They hadn't talked about anything that mattered. Kath had forced lightness into everything she said, calling him 'littl'un' and laughing nervously at the least opportunity.

'They've probably just forgotten you were coming,' she had told him more than once, even though they both knew that didn't explain the state of the house. 'They're probably off clubbing.' They had eaten noodles from the Cantonese Kitchen, even though Kath couldn't really afford it, as she had made sure to tell him. She fried some onions and mushrooms to go with it. Liam had felt much better after the food, his headache receding, a calmness reasserting itself. Before . . . . it had been as if there was a jabber of voices in his head, closing in on him, and he had been intensely aware of the city of human souls all around him.

They had waited by the telephones: Kath's hanging from the living-room wall, Liam's mobile open and ready on a coffee table.

There had been no calls, no knocks on the door from the police. No nothing.

He must have dozed again, because he woke to a terrified scream bursting out of the flat's one bedroom.

Kath!

He sat upright, feeling suddenly helpless, his arms trapped in the sleeping bag, its hood pulled tight round his face by the drawstring. For a moment, he felt as if he was being smothered, then he forced himself to get a grip. He took a steadying breath and worked a hand up to loosen the hood, then found the zip.

The bedroom door banged open and Kath staggered out, pale slug-like thighs lit yellow by the street lamp, a T-shirt swinging round her middle as she moved. Her eyes caught Liam's, and the whites burned gold in the room's eerie light.

She jerked away, flapped at the kitchen door, fumbled for a light.

He half expected someone – or something – to follow her from her room: whatever it was that had woken her screaming and given her those terrified animal eyes.

No. She must have been dreaming. Nightmares.

He heard water running, a cupboard banging, a rattle, a clatter of glass or china. Then he heard the feet of a stool being dragged across the lino.

He extracted himself from the sleeping bag and stood. Straightening his T-shirt and boxer shorts self-consciously, he paused to pull on a pair of jeans from his bag, then went through.

'What's up?'

She jerked and looked round. She can't have heard him come in. She was sitting on a tall wooden stool, elbows on the draining board by the sink. She let her head settle back into her hands. A mug sat on the ridged metal surface before her, and a white plastic pill bottle with the lid by its side. She tugged the hem of her T-shirt down.

Liam approached her cautiously, and stood leaning against the fridge. Tear tracks highlighted his sister's face.

'What's up?' he said again.

'I . . .' Her voice was a mere croak. She smacked the palm of one hand against the side of her head and slumped. 'It's hard to take,' she said weakly.

Was this guilt? Guilt that she had rebelled at school and then turned her venom on their parents before finally leaving to live on her own and ignoring them altogether? And now their parents had vanished . . . Liam had expected that she wouldn't care, but now he thought she must care a great deal indeed.

'They'll turn up,' he told her now. Somehow this didn't seem right. He didn't feel that he should have to be the one offering comfort and advice. 'They'll turn up, and when they do you can talk to them.' He almost added that it was never too late, but thought better of it. 'It'll be okay,' he finished lamely.

She was staring at him. Those same scared eyes.

He saw that she had barely calmed down at all.

'No,' she said. 'It's not them. It's this.' Her eyes flicked around the room, as if showing him what it was she couldn't take. 'It's *you*, littl'un.'

He stared at her, feeling as if the ground had been pulled from under his feet.

'It's *you* that I can't cope with . . . All the rest . . .' She waved a hand dismissively. 'But you . . . here . . . It's too much.' She smacked the side of her head again. 'Too much.'

She reached for the plastic bottle, hesitated and then

tipped another pill out. She washed it down with a gulp of water from her mug.

Liam stared at her. The mug had a picture of a smiling cow on it, with big pink udders and friendly eyes. She put the mug down and now he stared at it. Something normal. Something sane.

He didn't know what to say, what to think.

She was looking at him, sideways on. More tears were flowing down the crease between nose and cheek. 'I shouldn't feel . . . *this*,' she said. 'I should be able to cope. You're . . . my brother.' She jerked her head away and leaned low over the sink so that Liam thought she was about to throw up. Instead, she took a series of deep breaths.

She rubbed at her nose with the heel of her hand. Then she tipped her head back so that her face was lit by the yellow light coming in from the living room, the street lamp.

She looked at him, suddenly calm. Liam suspected that the pills must have started to work, whatever they were.

'I'm sorry,' she said, her voice lazy, distant. 'It's not you. It's me. I . . . have problems. It's just me. Go back to bed. Back to sleep. We'll talk in the morning.'

She drifted across the room then. As she passed him in the doorway, she reached up and brushed his cheek with the back of her hand, the first time they had touched as far as Liam could remember.

When she had gone, he switched off the light and went back to his borrowed, musty sleeping bag. He leaned back, his knees in the air and his feet on the arm of the sofa. He had always thought she had left home because she had rowed with their parents, but tonight changed all that. She had said it. She had said that she couldn't cope with him being there. She couldn't take it. Couldn't take *him*.

His sister hated him and yet right now she was all he had in the world.

The living-room window faced east and the morning sun woke him early. He reached out for his phone and checked it, but there were no messages. He lay back, holding the phone to his chest.

He looked round the room, realizing for perhaps the first time quite what a shabby existence his sister lived. An old TV, a tiny stereo. A vase of artificial flowers by the window. Up on the mantelpiece over the electric fire, he saw a couple of postcards. Southwold and La Rochelle. Liam had sent them to her last year, one a day trip and the other a holiday with Mum and Dad. She couldn't bear to have him here, yet she kept his postcards . . .

He glanced at her bedroom door, firmly closed, a barrier.

He wondered just when it was that the two of them had gone wrong, when they had become people who could no longer live in the same house.

He remembered the rows between his parents and Kath. Or rather, he remembered the aftermath, the angry silences, the sense that there were things left unsaid. He had been away a lot of the time, at NATS, and before that at a prep school in Cambridgeshire.

Earlier memories. Playing with Kath on a wide, sandy beach, somewhere in Norfolk. Blue skies and sandcastles, and later a picnic on a tartan travel rug spread across the crisp white sand. Christmases and birthdays stuck in his mind: happy family occasions with cakes and candles and presents to unwrap. All these memories seemed to run together in Liam's mind, much of the detail lost. It was like an album of family photos: they could have been anybody's, but they were his, his childhood, his family, his sister.

He didn't know when things could have started to break down.

He lay there quietly, trying to close down all the random noise in his head. It was often like this, back in Norwich. He pictured it as the city trying to burst in. All those voices, all those people crammed into the streets around him, a constant background jabber. His head was starting to pound again.

Much later, Liam heard sounds from the bedroom and then the door opened. Kath came out in black jeans and a crimson sweater, with a jolly smile on her face. He wondered how long she had been trying to force that expression into place. She hated him, he remembered.

She didn't say anything. She must have sensed his mood.

She went through to the kitchen and started to bang cupboards and crockery.

Liam dragged himself out of the sleeping bag, leaving it in a screwed-up heap on the floor. In the bathroom, he peered at himself in the mirror. Heavy black shadows were slung below his eyes, and his skin was pale, greasy. He decided it wasn't yet time for his fortnightly shave. He splashed cold water over his face, running wet hands through his hair to smooth it down and refresh his scalp.

There was a plate on the coffee table, mounded high with scrambled eggs, tomatoes from a tin, sausages. Kath stood behind the sofa, that forced smile on her face again. 'Eat up,' she said, waving a hand at the food.

'I . . .' Liam put a hand to his throbbing head. She was making an effort this morning, but he just didn't think he could eat.

'Go on,' she insisted. 'It'll do you good. It'll get you off to a good start. Sit down. Eat up.'

There was a tense edge to her voice. She seemed to be saying that if she could make the effort, then the least he could do was go along with it.

He sat on the edge of the sofa and stared at the plate. Kath handed him a knife and fork and stood just to one side, waiting for him to start.

He prodded at the egg, took a little on the fork and raised it to his mouth.

She was right. It smelled good, tasted good. It was just like the refectory food at NATS. He took another forkful, and another.

Soon the plate was clear. He sat back. 'Thanks,' he said. 'Aren't you . . .?'

She shook her head. 'I had toast,' she said.

His head was clear again, he realized. The food had made a big difference.

'So,' he said as Kath came to sit on a beanbag against the wall, 'what do we do?'

Kath shrugged. 'We sit back,' she said. 'All we can do is wait. Keep our heads down and wait.'

She was probably right, but it made Liam feel so

helpless! He felt that he should be out there, doing something. But what could he do? What did they know?

'You can stay here,' said Kath softly. 'As long as you need to.'

He looked at her, remembering last night. He couldn't work her out. He looked away again and tried to think what to do next.

The city seemed different today. It was nothing obvious. He stood on the narrow footbridge over Grapes Hill and looked down at the solid Saturday morning traffic. All these people in their cars, carrying on as normal. But Liam had emerged in a different and frightening world where all the rules seemed to have changed: his parents had vanished, their house had been ransacked, his sister couldn't bear to be with him. Yet for all these people in their cars and their ordinary lives it was all the same as ever. They didn't realize just how close they were to having their worlds turned upside down. Everyone was living on the knife-edge, but they just couldn't see it.

He hadn't known where he was heading when he went down the stairs from Kath's flat.

She stood at the top, telling him not to go. 'What if they . . . or someone . . . phones?' she said.

He had taken his mobile from his pocket and waved it at her. 'If anyone calls me I'll let you know. And if anyone calls here you can call me.'

Kath seemed resigned to just sitting by the telephone and waiting to see what happened. Their parents would call them, or someone would make contact, or the police would discover something. Liam couldn't do that, though. He couldn't just sit and wait.

Stepping outside had been like a great weight lifting, a blanket being pulled back from his eyes. He was able to breathe again. He hadn't realized quite how tense the atmosphere had still been between his sister and him, until he stepped out into the morning air.

Now, he stood and watched the traffic crawling past beneath him.

He turned away from the peeling green rails and went down the bridge to Upper St Giles Street, heading for the city centre.

A few minutes later he stood before the public entrance to the police station. It led into a gloomy waiting area with a high ceiling and posters on the walls. Liam approached the enquiries desk and an officer turned to look at him. He was a bulky man, with short ginger hair and a slight squint. 'Yes? What can I do for you?'

Liam hesitated. 'It . . . It's about an incident. Yesterday. My parents disappeared and the house was turned upside down. I stayed with my sister last night. There was a policeman – two. One in uniform and another in a suit. They took me to my sister's. They said they'd call but we haven't heard anything. I thought someone here might . . .'

He ground to a halt, realizing that he hadn't made much sense.

'Hold on a minute,' said the policeman. 'What's your name? Where do you live? Just give me some details and I'll find someone who can talk to you, okay?' He had a friendly manner, but Liam sensed that he probably thought he was mad.

'Connor. I'm Liam Connor. I live with my parents at 23 New Chapel Road, up near Mousehold Heath.'

The man scribbled this down on a memo pad, then picked up a telephone. 'Okay,' he said to Liam as he punched a number. 'Give us a minute and someone'll be through.'

Liam sat. He had a terrible feeling that it had been a mistake to come here. He felt guilty, accused.

A short time later, a tall, dark-haired man with a neat little moustache and a blue suit came out to the waiting area. 'Liam Connor? Come on through. I'm Detective Constable Parker.'

Liam followed him into an interview room and they sat across a table from each other.

'So tell me, Liam,' said DC Parker, 'what, exactly, happened yesterday?'

'I came home from school for the weekend,' Liam said. 'But when I got home, the place had been wrecked and my parents were missing. The police came and took me to my sister's. They said they'd find out what happened and let us know. We haven't heard anything, so I came here.'

'How old are you, Liam?'

'Fifteen.'

'Okay, Liam. Can you tell me who this policeman was? You told Bob on the desk that there was one in uniform and one in plain clothes. What were their names?'

'They never said.'

'What kind of car did they drive? Was it a marked police car?'

Liam shook his head. 'No, it was just a silver car, unmarked. A Ford Focus, I think.'

'What's your sister's name? Does she have a telephone?'

'Kath,' said Liam. He took out his phone to check her number, then turned it to show DC Parker.

'Okay, Liam. Give me a few minutes and I'll be back. Okay?'

Liam sat alone in the interview room.

Eventually, Parker returned. He didn't sit this time. Instead, he stood, leaning forward on the back of the chair opposite Liam. 'Right, Liam. I want you to be straight with me this time. Is that okay?'

Liam nodded, uncertainly, eyes fixed on the policeman's face.

'Is this some kind of a game, or are you telling the truth?'

Liam still stared. After a few seconds of silence, he said, 'What do you mean, "a game"?'

The policeman let the silence return for a few seconds more before he replied. 'I've just checked the system and spoken to some of my colleagues, and I'm puzzled.'

He was shaking his head slowly as he spoke. 'You see, Liam, there *was* no report of an incident at New Chapel Road yesterday. No missing persons report. No report about a house being vandalized. Nothing. We have no record of the police having attended the incident you describe.'

Liam realized he had been holding his breath. He let it go, breathed in again. What was this man telling him?

'As far as we're concerned, Liam, this incident never happened.'

4

You Can Never Go Back from Here

Sometimes, when you pull at a loose thread, nothing much happens. But there's always the danger that you have started something you might regret. The seam splits, the fabric separates. One thing leads to another. In less than twenty-four hours, Liam's world has unravelled. The familiar has become the strange. The known now seems unknowable. The safe has become dangerous, and one thing still leads on to many others.

'Go back to your sister, or your parents, or wherever,' DC Parker told Liam as they stood outside the police station. 'Go back and think about what you've told us. Think about what really happened. Then if there's anything to report, come back and ask for me. Okay, Liam? Do you understand?'

Liam felt that he was being told to just go back to his normal life, and stop telling tall stories. If only it could be that easy.

Head spinning, he walked a short way until he was on a small terrace, looking out over the striped canopies of the market. He sat on a wall and took out his phone. No messages. He tried his mother, his father. Nothing. He called Kath.

She answered on the first ring. 'Yes?'

'Kath. Me. Anything?'

'No. You okay, littl'un? You sound odd. What's happened?'

He opened his mouth to speak, to tell her . . . but he stopped. Not on the phone.

'Nothing,' he said. 'Just cold. Speak to you later.'

He zipped up his fleece. It was a grey day today, cooler than yesterday. He hadn't really noticed when he came out of the police station.

He tried to think. Either the 'policeman' at the house had been lying, or DC Parker had just now. But why? What were they covering up? It must be something his father was involved with, the work he would never tell anyone about. Government agencies, spies . . . or maybe he was just some kind of crook and things had finally gone wrong for him.

Liam couldn't believe any of that, though. His father was an ordinary man, who just happened to travel a lot and crack jokes about his work to make it sound exciting. There was nothing in their life that had ever suggested things would end up like *this*.

He considered getting on a bus out to the university. From there it was a ten-minute walk through the campus and over the river to the research park where lots of agricultural and medical research institutions had premises. But he'd never been to his mother's workplace. They had driven past a few times, but all that told him was how big and complex a site it was. He didn't even know which building she worked in, let alone where within that building. So going out to the research park was hardly going to gain him much.

He sat a little longer on the wall, looking out across the market. He had his phone cupped in his hands, just in case anyone rang.

Cold and numb, he moved on, walking aimlessly through the Saturday crowds to get his circulation going again. He couldn't work it out. Maybe Kath was right: all they could do was sit tight until something happened. Only then would they be able to make sense of any of it.

But there was one more thing he had to do. He was on Prince of Wales Road now, heading towards the river and the railway station. Soon he would be on Riverside Road and heading for home.

He had been putting this off, this walk, the same one he had done yesterday when he had jumped off the train full of the sense of freedom that a weekend at home would bring. He had put it off for fear of seeing it all again: the house, the mayhem. He had put it off for fear of what he might find too. Any clues he might have missed, anything that might hint that the violence had been directed at people as well as property.

There had been all kinds of reasons for putting it off.

But he could never have expected *this* . . .

New Chapel Road was just as it had always been. The houses set back from the street behind tidy front gardens.

The cars neatly slotted into their drives, each one shining as if it had had a Saturday morning wash and polish. The doves cooing from the trees and the rooftops.

Liam could almost find himself believing that nothing had happened.

The three eucalyptus trees flickered silvery-white in the breeze.

With a rising sense of dread, Liam crunched across the gravel drive. It was then that he realized why the front of the house seemed so bare. There were no curtains in the windows.

He stopped and peered into the front room.

It was empty. Stripped. There was no furniture. No carpets on the floor, no pictures on the wall. Not even a lightshade over the bare bulb.

He went to the door, but his key did not fit the shiny new Yale lock.

There were no windows at the side for him to look in, but he saw that the old trailer had gone. The back lawn was freshly cut. It had been shaggy and in need of a trim only the day before, a job his mother always put off and which Liam often ended up doing.

He peered into the kitchen, and it had been similarly stripped out. Even the units had gone, replaced by new ones with creamy white doors and metal handles. Liam stepped back, suddenly wondering whether he had come to the right house, the right *street*.

There was a tennis ball lodged in the gutter. Liam had knocked it there two weeks before, when he had been home for the bank holiday weekend. He had been playing tennis against the back wall and skied one.

He came back to the front and there was a man there, Mr Mendes from next door. Mr Mendes had always been a bit frightening, the kind of neighbour who had a shed full of children's balls that had ended up in his garden. Right now, he seemed a welcome and familiar figure.

'Hey,' Mr Mendes called as Liam emerged. 'What are you doing here?'

Liam looked at him, open-mouthed. He realized that his neighbour was staring at him like a complete stranger.

'I . . .'

'Go on, get out of there. I'll get the police on to you. There's neighbourhood watch, you know.'

Mr Mendes didn't have a clue who Liam was.

Liam looked from his neighbour to the house, and then back again. 'Who . . . who lives here? I thought . . .'

'It's empty, isn't it?' said Mr Mendes. 'As I expect you saw. Not for long, though. New tenants moving in tomorrow. I hope they're better than the last lot.'

'The last?'

'Bloomin' Pakis,' said Mr Mendes. 'Don't want their lot round here. Or yours. Go on, get out of here. I'll call the police.'

Liam walked past him, still stunned by what was happening. He felt like just sitting down in the middle of the pavement and giving up. What more could the world throw at him? How much more could he cope with?

It was well into the afternoon now, and Liam hadn't eaten since the breakfast Kath had cooked for him. He stopped at the market and bought a bag of chips. Around him, people talked and laughed and hurried about their business. He went and sat on some steps.

He was beginning to think that the police station had been the wrong kind of institution for him to visit this morning. He should have gone to the hospital and told them that the things he knew no longer matched the real world. He was sane enough to know that this was completely mad.

He was on his way back to Kath's flat. He knew that was where he would end up. But he didn't want to hurry. He wanted to put it off, delay everything as long as possible. He had a horrible feeling that when he got there and rang on the bell, a complete stranger would come to the door and ask who he was. Piece by piece, his life was being erased.

He took his phone out yet again. No messages. He tried his mother, his father, and all he got was their answering services.

He didn't dare try Kath. He wanted her still to be there. He didn't want to get the dead line that might hint that she too had been removed from his life.

A man was waiting in a white Volvo outside Kath's flat. The street was always heavily parked-up, but all the other cars were empty. Why would this man be sitting in his car unless he was waiting, or watching? He wore a dark suit and tie, and had dark glasses obscuring his eyes.

He saw Liam and immediately picked up a mobile phone and thumbed a number.

Liam walked on and considered just keeping going. But what about Kath? He should warn her. But he could call her on his mobile rather than going right up to the flat.

He hesitated and then it was too late.

The door to Kath's flat opened and another dark-suited man stood smiling at Liam. He was tall and thin, and deathly pale. 'Hello,' he said. 'You must be Liam. Come in, come in. Your sister's upstairs. She said you'd be along shortly. Come in. What are you waiting for?'

A car door thunked shut and he heard footsteps approach and stop just behind him.

'Who are you?' said Liam. 'What are you doing here?'

The man was still smiling. 'I'm Mr Smith,' he said. 'And my colleague behind you is another Mr Smith, although we're not related. We're investigating your parents' disappearance, Liam. We're here to help.'

'You're with the police?'

The man nodded. 'We're part of the official investigation.'

But there *was* no official investigation. According to DC Parker, the police knew nothing about it. Liam remembered his first encounter with the 'policeman' at his home. 'Do you have ID?' he asked.

The first Mr Smith nodded but made no move to show it.

Liam looked up to the living-room window. Kath was there, watching them. He raised his eyebrows and she jerked her head, telling him to come up, stop messing around.

Liam slumped his shoulders, dropped his head and trudged in past Mr Smith at the door. He didn't know what was going on. He wished it would all just stop. As he started to climb the stairs, the front door shut behind him, and then he heard Mr Smith following him up.

There was another man in the room, wearing a similar dark suit to the two Smiths. His grey hair was thin on top and he wore thick, black-framed glasses. He was sitting on the sofa, keying something into a notebook computer. He barely glanced up as Liam and the first Mr Smith entered.

Liam looked at Kath and she smiled at him. 'You okay?' she asked.

He shrugged.

'These men,' she continued. 'They're looking for Mum and Dad.'

'And you, Liam,' added Mr Smith. 'We were concerned when your sister said that you had gone off on your own in the city. You should be cautious at such a difficult time. At least, until we know the fate of your parents.'

That phrase had an ominous ring: 'the fate of your parents'.

'Where are they?' said Liam. 'What's going on?'

'Sit down, Liam,' said the man with the computer, waving a hand towards the other end of the sofa. The man had a soft voice and a Scottish accent. 'We want to talk to you. We want to find out what's happened.'

'Who are you?'

The man stared at Liam as he sat. 'You don't need to know who we are, lad. We're members of Special Intelligence, an agency which reports to the Home Office. We look after people like you. Let's leave it at that.'

Special agencies . . . What did the government have to do with all this?

Liam didn't like the man's stare, but he found that he couldn't look away. He was like a rabbit, transfixed by a car's headlights. He felt dizzy, felt as if the room was rushing round him. It took all his concentration to steady himself. How did the man do that?

'I went to the house,' Liam said. He felt the need to talk, to win these men's trust. It would be good if they were on his and Kath's side. 'Home. This morning. Someone had cleared it. Since yesterday. Everything was gone. The curtains, the furniture, the carpets, the pictures and books and kitchen units. They've mowed the lawn, although they didn't do the edges. They've wiped out any sign that we ever lived there. Apart from the tennis ball.' He chuckled at that. 'The one I hit up into the gutter a couple of weeks ago.'

He stopped to gather himself. Mr Smith gave him a glass of water and he took it, sipped, put it down on the coffee table. 'Our next-door neighbour came round and found me. Mr Mendes. "Mental Mendes" – remember, Kath? He didn't know me. He didn't recognize me. Everything's been wiped away . . . Even in Mr Mendes' head. What's going on?'

The two men exchanged a glance, and then the Scot spoke. 'It's an erasure,' he said. 'They've removed any evidence that your parents existed. It's going to make them very hard to track down, lad.'

Liam looked at him. He could see himself reflected in the man's thick glasses. 'Who are "they"?' he asked, not sure if he wanted to know the answer. 'Why would they want my parents erased? Why is a government agency investigating this?'

'You don't need to know, Liam.'

Liam nodded. It seemed fair enough that these men from Special Intelligence should only tell him what he needed to know. He felt that very strongly, all of a sudden.

'We want to know how *you* are, Liam. We were concerned. We thought you were in your sister's protection, but she let you out into the city.' As he said this, he darted a look at Kath, then returned his gaze to Liam. 'So how are you coping? You're under a lot of stress, right now, aren't you?'

Liam shrugged. 'I'm okay,' he said.

'Come here,' the man said. 'Lean closer.'

Liam did so. The man reached up and ran a hand over Liam's scalp. He nodded. Then he put something to Liam's left eye, a kind of frame that sat in the eye socket, holding a lens that made everything blur. A face loomed close, black-framed eyes suddenly snapping into focus, magnified so that every tiny movement looked seismic.

The man sat back, removing the device from Liam's eye. He keyed something into his notebook. 'Everything seems stable so far,' he said to the first Mr Smith, who was watching intently from the doorway.

'What's all this got to do with . . . with what's happened?' asked Liam. He felt a little detached from what was going on, as if he was watching it happen rather than taking part.

'Everything,' said the man in the glasses. 'It has everything to do with it, lad. Everything connects, even the unconnected. You'd be surprised.'

The man snapped his computer shut. 'We want you to stay here, Liam. Do you understand? And if anything happens, we'll talk again.'

'But . . . how do I let you know if anything happens?'

The man smiled, the first time he had done so. 'Oh, Liam, don't you worry about that. If we're needed we'll be on hand. We always are.'

His gaze locked into Liam's for one last time. 'I think you need to get some rest now, Liam. You've had a lot of excitement today. You need to compose yourself.'

Liam nodded. The man was right. His words, in their soft Scottish tone, made perfect sense. Liam's eyelids were heavy – too heavy to hold open.

The man stood and helped Liam swing his legs up on to the sofa. Moments later, Liam was in darkness again.

5

Out On Your Own

Liam slept. He curled up on the sofa with his knees tucked under his chin, his hands shoved into his face. Babies in the womb curl up in this manner. It's the most compact, tidy way for them to fit into such a confined space. Animals in shock curl up like this too. It's a defence mechanism, a means of trying to shut out the horrors of the world and retreat into a safe, sheltered, enclosed space.

Liam woke, stiff and aching. He had been curled up tightly on the sofa, a position he didn't like, one which made him uncomfortable.

The flat was in gloom, the curtains drawn even though it was still light outside. Kath had the radio on in the kitchen, voices talking in tinny, scratchy tones.

Liam took his phone from his pocket and flipped it open. Still nothing.

He stretched, his legs poking out over the end of the sofa. He remembered Mr Mendes at the house, the look on his face . . . the complete lack of recognition. The empty house, talk of new tenants. How could there be new tenants when Liam's parents owned the house? He remembered the shock as DC Parker told him that there was no record of any police investigation into what had happened at Liam's home the day before. And the Special Intelligence men here, the two Mr Smiths and the nameless Scot who seemed to be in charge.

At this, Liam stiffened and levered himself upright. He peered around the room, but it was empty now. No sign of this afternoon's visitors. He settled back into the sofa.

All these incidents . . . Everything that had happened over the last two days seemed like scenes from a bad dream, a fevered hallucination.

Maybe he had just woken up from it.

But he knew that couldn't be true. If it was, then why wake up here and not back at home, or even back at NATS?

Everything seemed detached. Unreal. He wondered again if he had gone mad. There was that buzzing in his head again, that sense of the world closing in.

He got up and went through to the kitchen where Kath sat on the high wooden stool, idly flicking through a magazine. She looked up and smiled awkwardly.

'I'm hungry,' said Liam. He found it hard to say much more.

She nodded. She was looking after him. She made him some food – beans, microwave chips, an omelette – and brought it through to him in the living room. She watched as he ate it, and afterwards he felt calmer again. This was what they called comfort eating, he supposed. Food to settle the jangly state of his thoughts. Food to straighten his head.

★

He woke again, and it was morning.

He remembered the evening, another awkward time of a few exchanged words, of two people uncomfortable together. Familiar, yet strangers.

And the night. Dozing and waking, over and over, unsettled by the street lamp and the noises of the city. Kath had been awake through the night too. He could tell. He remembered the previous night, her outburst, her hatred. Nights seemed to be worst for her: she seemed more exposed then.

She cooked him breakfast again. They hardly exchanged a word. It was as if they had exhausted all their small talk and had run out of anything more substantial to say.

Afterwards, calmer, he gathered his things into his weekend bag.

Kath leaned by the window, half looking out into the street and half watching Liam. 'What are you doing?' she said.

'I'm going back to school. It's Sunday. I have to be back by six. I might as well go this morning.'

She looked anxious, eyes widening. 'You can't,' she told him. 'You heard what they said. You have to stay here, with me, until this is all over.'

'What is there to wait here for?' said Liam. In the night he had realized that Kath wasn't the only thing in his life left . . . unerased. There was NATS too. There were Anders and Hayley and all the others. Skiver too. 'If I don't get back on time they'll mark it against me. I can't get kicked out of NATS.' He had been about to add that she, of all people, must know how easy it was to get turned out if you don't make the grade, but he stopped himself.

'You can't go back to that place,' said Kath. 'NATS is the last place you want to be right now. Ever.'

Her failure at NATS still hurt, clearly.

'They want me,' said Liam. 'I belong there.'

That hurt her. No one at NATS woke in the night to tell him how they couldn't stand him to be around.

He checked his wallet for his return ticket.

Kath hadn't moved from the window. 'They'll be watching,' she said. 'They'll be looking out for you.'

'Who?' said Liam. 'Who are "they", Kath? What do they want with us?'

She shrugged. 'They were here yesterday, weren't they? Special Intelligence. They told you they were always around. Look out for yourself, littl'un, you hear?'

She still stood by the window. She wasn't going to come across the room. No goodbyes, no farewell hugs. She couldn't stand to be near him.

Liam nodded. 'Look after yourself too,' he said. He didn't understand, but he knew his sister had problems of her own. The night terrors, the erratic behaviour, the pills. He slung his bag from his shoulder and took his phone from his pocket. 'I'll call if I hear anything,' he said.

She nodded. 'Me too.'

She stayed by the window as he went to the doorway, then he was heading down the narrow staircase to the front door.

Outside, on his own, he was aware that she was watching from above, but he didn't glance up. He paused by the door and looked along the street. It was thickly parked-up as usual, but there was no sign of the white Volvo, no sign of anyone sitting in a car, watching and waiting.

He ducked his head and went out across the road to the far pavement. Walking along towards Unthank Road, he glanced back but Kath was no longer visible in the window.

He waited for a long time outside the station, watching the taxis arriving and leaving, the people heading to and from their cars. The station had a grand entrance, a brick extension with stone-edged arches where taxis picked up and dropped off passengers. Up above the entrance, the clock hands edged round.

This was the only way in. It would be easy for them – whoever *they* really were – to watch.

He waited until another taxi arrived, and while its passengers climbed out and sorted their bags, Liam ducked his head and darted through into the station. He stopped by a cluster of telephone booths and looked around anxiously. Nothing.

He felt a bit foolish then. Was all this cloak-and-dagger stuff really necessary? Why would anyone be watching for him?

But Kath had seemed convinced. And he remembered the three visitors yesterday. They had been deadly serious about their business, whatever that business might be. He looked up at the departures board, even though he knew the trains left at ten past the hour.

He had twenty-five minutes to wait.

He headed down Platform Two to the far end, where two men with notebooks and cameras stood. He wanted to be as far away from the main part of the station as possible. He dropped his bag and slumped to sit cross-legged beside it. The two trainspotters gave him a glance then returned to their conversation.

He followed the time passing on his wristwatch, all the while staring back along the platform to the ever-changing mix of people around the ticket office, the shop, the telephones and coffee shop. For some reason he was expecting to see the men in suits, the Mr Smiths or maybe the 'policeman' from Friday. It could be anybody, he realized. These trainspotters who barely paid him any attention might at any time reveal that they knew him, that they had been waiting for him in case he decided to leave the city. That woman, walking across to the telephones. She had glanced towards Liam and the trainspotters. Could she be the one who had been set to watch the station? Was she calling the Smiths right now as he watched?

A rumble on the tracks and the train was approaching, then roaring past. It stopped and people emerged. There weren't many travellers today, not on a Sunday.

As these people walked away from Liam, others walked in his direction, looking up at the train, deciding which door to enter by, where they would sit.

Liam stared at them.

He should move, he knew. He climbed to his feet and walked up to the train.

Just then, he saw a man in a suit and dark glasses approaching, a black attaché case dangling from one hand. Liam stopped. Was this it?

The man looked at him, then past him. He walked on by, not breaking his stride, and then entered the first carriage.

Liam walked further along the train and joined a carriage in the middle. There were lots of empty seats. He chose a pair of seats near the door, dumped his bag by the window and sat in the aisle seat, where he would be able to see along the carriage.

Again, he felt a strange mixture of foolishness and of being terribly exposed and vulnerable. Was all this really necessary? But at the same time, if it *was*, then did he really think that his childish games of hide-and-seek, of catch-me-if-you-can, would be enough to outwit professionals?

He was only doing his best.

He slumped in his seat. He looked along the carriage at the handful of other passengers, speculating about who they were and what they were doing. What else could he do?

He could think. He could go over and over in his head all the things that had happened, all the incidents that made no sense.

They had to make sense, though. They had happened. His parents had vanished. The house had been trashed, then cleared. The fake policemen had been there. The Special Intelligence people had visited Kath's flat. Mental Mendes had failed to recognize him. Kath couldn't stand to have her own brother in the flat.

These things were fact. They might make no sense. It might be impossible to see what connected them. But the one thing that bound them together was that they had happened to Liam this weekend.

So why him? Why Liam?

Maybe that was where his thinking was being led astray.

Maybe it wasn't just Liam. Maybe he was a peripheral figure, a bit-part player in someone else's story – his parents' story, perhaps. That might explain why it made so little sense: he was only seeing a very small part of the picture. Why should it centre around him? It made more sense that he was witnessing events that focused on someone more important.

But that still left him struggling for an explanation.

Things had changed around him. What had the Scot called it? Erasure. Bits of Liam's life were being erased all around him.

One question worried him almost as much as anything else: were the changes in his head, or in the outside world?

If they were taking place in his head, that meant that at least some of his memories were false, that his understanding of his existence could not be relied on. It meant that he was insane. But if these changes were really taking place in the outside world, that might be more worrying altogether . . . What was he up against, if they, that mysterious *they*, could manipulate everything to this extent? All evidence of entire lives was being deleted. The memories of people like Mr Mendes were being changed and blanked out.

They were rearranging the world around Liam.

Yes, that was the most disturbing possibility of all.

The train rolled past the big warehouses and grain silos at Diss and pulled up at the station. Liam looked along the carriage to see who was getting out. A woman with two small children. An old Chinese man.

Liam stood, moved towards the open door and stepped out. No one else from his carriage made a late move to leave the train. He was confident now that he was not being followed. He had a fifteen-minute wait until the two-carriage local train set out on the East Suffolk Line. He bought a chocolate bar and a packet of crisps from the machine and went to wait on a bench surrounded by tubs and hanging baskets.

He checked his phone, something that had become a reflex action, and always with the same result. No missed calls. No messages. He sat back and waited.

Whether all these events centred around him, or they were merely part of someone else's story, it was Liam's life being messed with. It was Liam's parents who were missing, his home that had been wiped away. He had to hang on to what was left.

And he had to work out how to fight back.

Wolsey station was at the end of the branch line. It was a small, red-brick building, sitting across the end of the single track. Liam walked through the building, the glass-panelled ticket office to his left, and emerged on the pavement.

He didn't have the taxi fare to get back to NATS and there were no buses on Sundays. Normally, his parents would have given him the money for a taxi, but he could hardly have asked Kath . . .

He shouldered his bag and set out on the long walk. Passing through the small seaside town's dense terraced streets, he could soon see the Mere. Wolsey sat at the top of a shingle point that jutted south for a few miles to the derelict army base, Wolsey Camp. A wide, muddy creek wound between the point and the mainland and here at Wolsey it opened out into a broad, shallow, saltwater lake:

the Mere. Across the water, Liam could see trees, fields, and in the distance the two flags which flew from the roof of the main NATS building.

He felt a sudden surge of pride at the sight. This was his place, his school. Until now, he hadn't quite realized how much he had been hanging on to that thought: that despite everything, he always had NATS.

In his line of sight it was about a mile to NATS, but because of the Mere and the winding creek that cut inland from Wolsey, he had a walk of about six miles ahead of him.

He set out, glad that it was another cool, grey day. He remembered the trip out from the school to the station on Friday, riding on the back of Jake's motorbike. It had only taken a few minutes. He remembered the wind rushing by, yanking at his hair, roaring in his ears. He remembered the sense of complete freedom, the last time he had felt anything remotely like freedom. It had been like reaching the peak of a roller coaster before crashing down the steepest of slopes.

He had hoped that someone might pass him in a car: a teacher, perhaps. Someone who would recognize him and stop to give him a lift the rest of the way. But the roads were quiet this afternoon.

When NATS came into view again, Liam's legs and shoulders were aching, his feet sore. He had removed his fleece and tied it round his waist. He was thirsty and tired and hungry. He just wanted to get back into his room and flop.

He reached the wrought-iron gates and looked up the long straight drive, lined with poplars. The school building sat at the far end, always a striking sight along this avenue of ancient trees. There were people there, someone on the steps, some others walking across in front of the building. Normal life . . . the very idea of a normal existence seemed foreign to Liam right now.

He paused to put on his school tie, then trudged up the drive.

Two girls sat on the steps, studying something on the small screen of a mobile phone. Rebecca Mills and Hannah Jessop. They barely glanced up at Liam as he turned to the right to follow the gravel road round the side of the building. Beyond them, a blond senior Liam half recognized looked across at him. He was a French kid, a loner. The seniors didn't tend to mix with the main school. This boy watched Liam curiously as he passed.

Emerging from the deep shade of the yew trees, Liam could see that there was a cricket match going on. He considered going over to watch, but the thought of his room proved too much of a temptation.

He came to the entrance to Sherborne House, which occupied this end of the main dormitory wing of the school building. He flipped the perspex cover of the keypad and thumbed the security code to get in.

When he pushed at the door it stuck firm, and he realized he hadn't heard the soft click of the lock releasing.

He thumbed the number again, more carefully this time, but still the door wouldn't give.

Even now, he wasn't too concerned. Sometimes, if you got the number wrong and tried again, the lock wouldn't respond, as if it was still stuck after the first try.

He paused for a few seconds, plenty of time for it to clear.

When he tried again and the lock refused to release, he started to panic.

It was happening again.

He needed help. He needed somebody to step in and tell him it was all some awful mistake. Someone to sort it all out.

He heard voices. Laughter.

There were some girls sitting out on the grass just round the corner. One of them was Hayley.

He approached them warily.

For a long time, they didn't look up, and in all those long seconds Liam was able to cling to the hope that this wasn't going to happen, that another part of his life had not been erased.

And then they looked up. First Laryssa, then Tsuki and Naomi.

And finally Hayley.

She looked at him, first fixing his eyes and then her glance skipping over his features. There was no recognition in her look.

'Hayley?' he said.

She frowned. Just as you would if a stranger came up and greeted you by your name.

'Do I . . .?' she said, letting the words tail off.

'It's me. Liam.'

Someone said something he didn't quite catch, and Hayley looked away, pulled a face, and the girls started to snigger.

Liam backed away. His world had been wiped out.

6

Unexploded

Schools, these days, are high-security places. Pupils carry ID cards and all visitors have to be filtered through a central reception area. It's only sensible, in times like these.

A school like the National Academy for the Talented and Special has even more reason to be careful. The parents of many of its pupils work for the Ministry of Defence, the armed forces or the diplomatic service, and they need to know that their offspring will be working and studying in a safe environment. So, relaxed as NATS may appear on the surface, it is, in fact, a closely monitored, highly secure institution.

Nothing goes unseen or unheard.

Liam turned away from the four girls on the grass. He remembered thinking he must be playing a part in someone else's story, but . . . first home and now NATS . . . This was *his* world being wrecked. It was *his* story. But what was the connection between what had happened at home and now at NATS? What was being done to him?

He retreated round the corner of the building and that was where he met Mr Willoughby. The principal was standing there with two men Liam did not know. If this hadn't been a school, he would have taken them for some kind of security guards. They were taller than the principal, with broad, muscular shoulders and a way of standing that reminded Liam of big cats poised for action.

Willoughby smiled. 'Liam Connor,' he said. 'Welcome back to the academy.'

So the principal still knew him. Somehow, Liam didn't find that a comfort right now, as the two guards moved slightly to either side of Willoughby, blocking the path.

Liam's mind raced, and he didn't like where it was heading.

'Principal Willoughby,' said Liam. 'What's going on? What's happening?'

Willoughby spread his hands, as if to show that he had nothing to hide. 'Nothing's happening,' he said. 'It's all over. You're back. We want to welcome you. We want to resume our work with you.'

They weren't working 'with' Liam. They were working *on* him . . .

Liam suddenly saw himself as a laboratory animal, with Willoughby the scientist in charge. Was Willoughby responsible for it all? Was he the one pulling all the strings?

'Come along, Connor,' said Willoughby. 'My two friends here will help you in with your bag. We have new accommodation for you.'

The two guards approached Liam. The path narrowed here and so they came in single file.

Liam let his bag drop from his shoulder and caught it by the handhold. All the time from Wolsey, those six long miles, he had cursed its bulk and weight. Such a big bag, just for a weekend at home! Now he raised it to his chest. They were going to help him with his bag. Okay then . . .

He hurled it at the lead guard, with all the strength he could muster.

The man was taken by surprise. He saw what had happened late, saw the bag flying through the air at his head.

He cursed, raised his hands, swung his head back.

The bag struck him in the face, knocking him back into the arms of the second guard, and the two of them fell in a heap.

Liam turned and ran.

His tired and aching body howled in protest, but he ignored it, and sprinted as fast as he could. Along the path at the side of the building and out on to the grass again. Right through the middle of the startled group of girls, feeling a sudden sense of angry betrayal that Hayley still did not know who he was.

Out on the playing field, the cricket match was still going on. Liam swung right, into the stand of pines and evergreen oaks. He heard voices behind him, shouting, arguing.

He looked back and saw one of the guards, far closer than he had expected.

Every breath tore at the lining of his throat, and his lungs ached with the effort.

Gorse blazed yellow all around him in a sudden burst of sunlight breaking through the clouds. He twisted and darted unexpectedly to the left. It would look like he had plunged into the heart of the gorse, but there was a narrow track here, a path through the thicket.

He ran, and the dry green spines of the gorse scraped and snagged at his trousers, but he didn't slow.

The scrub opened out again and he ran on, taking another narrow path through a blackthorn thicket. This was a completely different world now, the ground beneath his feet sandy, held together by a tight, rabbit-cropped mat of grass. The school was out of sight, and the playing fields. He could neither see nor hear his pursuers now, but he knew that he had to keep going.

The blackthorn cleared and he was in an open, sandy area at the foot of a stand of pines. There were black patches here, encircled by big stones, where someone had broken the rules and lit fires. Like any other pupil at NATS, Liam knew all the places you could hide out in the school grounds. Places to smoke and hang out with friends away from the staff, places to come with a girlfriend, or just to be on your own.

He cut across between the tall, bare pine trunks and followed another trail through the gorse, slowing to an exhausted jog now.

Eventually, he came to another group of pine trees, on an old dune overlooking the creek.

He stopped for a rest. This was where Greasey Davies told them he'd spied on Miss Carver last summer. He'd seen her skinny-dipping in the creek and then sunbathing on a towel on the wet sand as the tide went out. It had become a popular meeting place for the boys for the rest of Summer Term, but no one had ever seen Miss Carver here again.

The tide was halfway now. It was coming in, Liam guessed, although it was hard to tell. Across the creek he could see the towering banks of shingle of Wolsey Point. Further along to the right, he could see the broken shell of the watchtower, one of the ruins of the old army camp. The place had been important during the Second World War, one of a string of bases along this coast that had been used in developing the first radar systems. It had been abandoned for twenty years or so now, and the place had become a wildlife haven, managed by the Point Preservation Trust.

The sun bathed the Point in vivid gold, against the retreating dark clouds. It really had turned into a beautiful evening.

Liam headed down to the strip of hard sand at the water's edge. He was heading north, upcreek. If he carried on, he would come to an area where the creek opened out into the Mere, flanked on this side by a wide area of saltmarsh. He would come to the road to Wolsey eventually, and he would have to hope they weren't watching it, waiting for him to reappear.

The punt gave him another option.

It was there ahead of him, dragged up on to the sand. It was a flat-bottomed punt, turned upside down so that it wouldn't catch rainwater. He tipped it up and saw that there were oars underneath.

He looked at the creek. It was about thirty metres wide

here and the current didn't seem too strong. He looked all around, but there was no sign of anyone.

He turned the punt the right way up, put the oars inside, went to the prow and dragged it slowly down to the water. When he reached the creek, he went to the back and pushed.

He got it most of the way in, gave it a final shove and then jumped aboard. With his extra weight, it grounded at the rear. He climbed out and pushed again, going into the water up to his knees before scrambling back into the punt.

The little vessel sat there, turning idly in the current so that the prow pointed south. The tide was coming in, but the surface current still flowed southwards, out to sea. The two seemed to balance right now, allowing the punt to stay pretty much where it was while Liam worked out how to get the oars into the rowlocks.

He started to row. At first he scooped the water too shallowly and went nowhere. Then he started to get the hang of it and the punt headed out into the channel.

As he rowed, he faced the mainland, and so he could see the school flags: a Union flag and a European Union flag. His slow progress across the water seemed to be emphasizing the fact that he was leaving all that behind: what he had understood to be his world.

The punt grounded on the far bank and, looking back, he saw that the surface current had dragged him south along the creek so that he had crossed at a sharp diagonal.

He scrambled to the prow of the punt and jumped out on to dry land. He was tempted just to leave the punt to float away into the North Sea, but he couldn't. He had to protect his options, and it was possible that he might need to use the punt again.

Exhausted, he forced himself to haul the punt up on to the shingle: no easy task, as the stones kept giving under his feet and the bank here was steeper than on the other side.

Eventually, he managed to pull the punt up above where he judged the high-water mark to be. He turned, on his hands and knees, and crawled up the shingle bank, sliding back with each upward move, before finally reaching the top. There was a flat area here, covered with brittle, dried moss.

He crawled across it until he was out of sight of the far bank, and then he slumped, face down, the moss prickling his cheek.

Liam woke, his throat dry, his face itching, his head pounding.

It was mid-evening now and the sun was low in the western sky.

He rolled on to his side, then sat up, hugging his knees to his chest.

He was alone in the middle of nowhere, and that part of the world which had not tried to forget him had turned against him.

Of more immediate concern, he was hungry and thirsty and soon it would be night. He was just as powerless over the first two of these as he was over the bigger picture: there was no food or drink out here.

But there was shelter, after a fashion.

The punt crossing had brought him further down the Point, so that the ruined buildings of the old camp were much closer than he had expected.

He walked for a few minutes across the shingle. The stones were more tightly packed here, but still difficult to walk on. Every so often, gulls hauled themselves into the air, screeching at him until he was past. He came to an area where the shingle was covered with a tight mat of creeping silvery-green vegetation with white, bell-like flowers, and smaller, pin-head blue flowers with white centres. The going was easier here as he trod the flowers underfoot.

He came to a concrete road and followed it.

A line of posts bearing a single strand of barbed wire cut across the road and the surrounding shingle. A battered yellow sign warned: DANGER.

Liam ducked under the wire.

The watchtower loomed up into the evening sky to his right. It was only a shell: a supporting metal post in each corner and a framework marking the level of the platform where the guards had once sat. The steps up to it had long since collapsed, and the floors too.

Clustered round the watchtower were some ruined buildings. To one side there was some kind of hangar, collapsed at one end and open to the elements, and round it a small group of concrete huts and garages. Further along was a big block-like building with gravel heaped up against its walls. To the other side, there was a row of single-storey brick buildings with doors and windows boarded over. These might once have been living quarters, Liam guessed.

Or maybe offices. They looked more inviting than the hangar and garages, at least.

Beyond that, out on the Point, there were more buildings, but Liam didn't feel up to trekking any further. He had sought out shelter and found it. He wanted to stop now. He wanted to sit down and try to get things straight in his head.

He tried the first building, and the board over the door came away easily.

It was gloomy inside but, as his eyes adjusted, the bare, stripped-out interior, empty and abandoned as it was, reminded him painfully of the last time he had seen his home.

The floor was concrete, covered in drifts of sand and shingle which must have blasted in through the gaps between boards and door and window frames.

Exhausted, Liam sat, leaning against the cold brick wall.

He took out his mobile to check for messages, wondering whether to call Kath or not. He flipped it open and its small screen lit up. No signal.

He really was on his own.

The night was bitterly cold, but Liam was delirious. He slept fitfully, uncomfortably, waking from vivid dreams, one moment feverish, the next chilled to the marrow. His head ached, a relentless, pounding pain behind his eyes. And his empty stomach burned.

He woke with a violent screeching cry filling his head.

He jerked upright, and bolts of pain stabbed through his stiff body.

The cry came again, and he realized it was a gull, welcoming the new day from the low roof of the building. He looked up and saw that there were wide holes in the roof, and blue sky high above. A white head appeared in one of these gaps, a heavy yellow beak. The head drew back and the gull gave its cry once more.

Liam went outside.

He propped the board up over the doorway again, and then set out on the concrete road, heading north towards Wolsey.

Soon, he came to the barbed-wire fence again and ducked under it. Further along, he came to another sign. 'DANGER,' it read. 'UNEXPLODED ORDNANCE.'

He had been lucky, he supposed. If so, it was for the first time in days.

7

What's Good for You

Sometimes, it is possible to be a prisoner without there being any locks on the door or bars on the window. You may not even realize that you are constrained.

Sometimes, though, the cage can help to clarify matters.

The Point narrowed here as the Mere opened out on Liam's left, the water sparkling in the morning sun.

And all the way across the narrow neck of the Point, cutting off the camp from Wolsey and its surroundings, stretched a high, chain-link fence.

Liam came to it and leaned forward so that it took his weight. The fence stretched above his head. At the top, an extension jutted out on the north side, metal arms with three strands of razor wire stretched tight. Off to the left, the fence dropped down into the Mere, and to the right it stretched down into the angry waters of the North Sea.

Liam slumped to his knees, then sat back on the shingle.

He should have expected something like this. He had seen enough signs warning about the dangers of the Point: unexploded bombs, contaminated and derelict buildings, concealed entrances to pits and other under-ground facilities.

Of course they would want to keep the public out.

Beyond the fence, he could see the wooden building that housed the local sailing club, and the network of yachts and jetties that spread across that part of the Mere. Principal Willoughby kept a boat here, he knew, and that thought put him even more on edge. He could hear the randomly rhythmic clanking of the boats' rigging, like Alpine cowbells. A short row of coastguards' cottages sat diagonally across the top of the Point, and Liam could see someone outside one of them, doing something to a pale car.

Beyond the cottages, where the Point joined the main-land, was the town itself. Two- and three-storey houses crowded together among the trees, each building painted either white or in subtly differing shades of blue, red, pink and yellow.

He was so close . . .

Liam had been walking on the tight-packed stones in the central strip of the Point. Now he clambered to his feet and moved across to the concrete road. There was a gate here, but it was just as high as the fence and secured with a heavy padlock and chains. They must use this for access when the preservation trust people came out to work on the Point. But they made sure to lock up after themselves.

Just then, Liam saw something that reinforced his sense of hopelessness. On the other side of the fence, the grass was cropped close to ground level, and little round rabbit droppings were scattered all about. On this side of the fence, the grass grew in tall tussocks. If even the rabbits couldn't get through or under the fence, what chance did Liam have?

The headache was back, and Liam's throat was dry and sore. Each step left him dizzy, the world spinning precariously.

This place . . . the Point . . . it was a desert. It was surrounded by seawater, and the few pools he found were all salty. Rain, when it came, would just drain away through the sand and stones. As for food, he could probably make a meal of raw gulls' eggs, but even the thought made his stomach heave.

He came to the wide area of dry moss, just above the gravel shelf where he had grounded the punt.

It was still there, the oars resting inside.

The sun was blazing down on him now, reinforcing his sense of being marooned in a desert. He needed to rest, but he knew he should do so in the shade.

He took several deep breaths and tried desperately to work some saliva into his mouth.

After a few more seconds, he slithered down the steep shingle wall to the punt. After another pause to gather himself, he stood, went to the boat and started to heave it into the water.

He had intended to row upcreek to the Mere, but the current was too strong. He had not thought to check the tide, but now, out in the middle of the channel, it was clearly dragging him downstream towards the sea. He had only wanted to get as far as the fence, but however hard he hauled on the oars it was no good.

Exhausted, he dug one oar deep into the water, trying to use it to steer. Gradually, the punt began to drift towards the far side of the creek.

A few minutes later it grounded and Liam struggled out on to the narrow sandy bank. Again, he made himself drag the boat out of the water, and then he collapsed back into a bed of coarse grass.

It wasn't quite sleep that he found, but a feverish drifting that lasted for much of the morning. In those short times when his head was relatively clear, he found himself wondering that just one day without food or drink could do this to him.

Clouds had covered the sun by the time he was able to gather himself and sit upright.

He looked around. He recognized the group of trees here. This was where school legend had it that Miss Carver did her skinny-dipping. The narrow trail from these trees led up through the gorse to Senior House and the sports pavilion.

He had to keep pausing to rest as he threaded his way up through the trees and then the gorse. He had to keep taking breaks, leaning against a tree if there was one nearby, taking deep breaths. He had to keep his goal in mind: the tap on the rear wall of the pavilion.

At the edge of the trees, he paused to put his tie on again, in the hope that if anyone spotted him he might at least look as if he belonged here. There was a PE lesson going on out in front of the pavilion, a group of Year Sevens in the cricket nets.

It was only a short distance from the trees to the back

of the pavilion, and Liam decided to stroll across as if he was meant to be there.

He stepped out from the trees and immediately felt exposed. He hesitated, then strode out towards the pavilion. Everything seemed so normal. The voices, the occasional shouted instruction from Mr Hughes. The regular, hollow knocks of cricket balls on willow.

But Liam knew that the so-called normal world had never existed. It had been a skin, a thin covering over a world horribly more complex and frightening than he could have imagined.

He reached the building and the tap. A hose was attached, so Liam unscrewed it.

He turned the tap on and marvelled at the gush of beautiful, clear water. He scooped his hands under the chilly flow, raised the water to his lips and drank.

It was so cold it almost burned his parched throat. He took another double handful.

Then he squatted, tipped his head sideways and let the water flow directly into his open mouth. He splashed water over his scalp and face, aware that it was soaking into his shirt and trousers.

Eventually, he turned the tap off and sat back on the grass, realizing too late that the ground was wet from the running water.

Only now did he think to take his phone from his pocket. He flipped it open. No messages. No calls missed while he had been out of reach of the signal.

And then he heard a clattering sound as someone dropped something metal inside the pavilion.

Instantly on his feet, Liam crept along the back of the building. A frosted window was partly open and he looked in through the gap.

He was peering into the small canteen area where the catering staff prepared teas and snacks for matches with visiting teams. There were squirts of white foam over one of the work surfaces. Someone was cleaning.

Liam glanced over his shoulder, but there was no one watching him. He looked back into the canteen and saw that it was Jake, the catering assistant, a cigarette hanging out of the corner of his mouth as he swiped a cloth through the foam.

Liam considered his options.

The safest was to slip away from the pavilion, find one of the many paths through the trees to the creek and head up to the road into Wolsey.

But he wanted to find out what was happening to him.

Weird things had taken place both in Norwich and here at NATS . . . They *must* be connected somehow. He wanted to know what had happened to his parents, and he wanted to understand why his friends no longer seemed to know who he was; why Principal Willoughby *did* recognize him but had suddenly tried to trap him. Was Willoughby really behind it all in some way, as he had thought earlier?

Would Jake know anything about what was going on here? Even if Liam had been erased from his memories too, Jake might be able to tell him something useful.

'Jake,' he said, plunging in the moment he had made his decision. 'Jake — over here at the window.'

Jake looked up, narrowing his eyes as he spotted Liam through the gap. He came over, opened the window and leaned there, tapping the ash from his cigarette against the frame. 'Yeah?' he said, straightening his long black fringe with his free hand and a bobbing motion of his head.

Liam had stepped back as the window swung open. Now he studied Jake. Were there any signs of recognition there?

'I . . .' Liam stopped. He hadn't worked out what he was going to say.

'What you after?'

'Do you . . . do you know who I am?'

Jake intensified his look. 'This a joke or something? You lost your memory?'

Liam shook his head. 'No. Not me. But . . .' He shrugged. How to explain, without having to explain too much?

'Why shouldn't I know you?' said Jake. 'You're that kid, ain't you? Finished at the school last Friday. I gave you a lift to the station, didn't I? I might work skivvying in the kitchens, but I ain't stupid.'

So they hadn't done anything to Jake's memories of Liam, then, although he appeared to think Liam had left altogether on Friday, rather than just gone home for the weekend. Liam didn't know if that was good or bad. The only other person here who knew who he was had been Willoughby . . .

Liam eyed his escape route across the narrow strip of rough ground to the trees.

'What're you doing back here, then?' Jake nodded towards Liam and added in a softer voice, 'You look like you've been sleeping rough – you okay, kid?'

Liam shrugged. 'I'm starving,' he said. 'I feel . . . rotten. I came here to get water.' He hesitated, then continued, 'And to see if I could work out what's going on here.'

Jake didn't seem surprised by what Liam was saying. 'What, here at the National Academy for the Twisted and Spooky?' He chuckled. 'I've been here two years, an' I ain't worked it out yet. I just keep my head down and do what they pay me for. I ignore all the freakish stuff.'

'Freakish?'

Jake chuckled again. 'I'll tell you later. Listen. We don't keep food here, but I can get you some. You want to meet up when I've finished? I'll be done at four.'

He must have seen Liam's expression change to one of suspicion. 'It's okay,' he said. 'I'm not setting you up. I went on the run myself when I was about your age. I know what it's like.'

As he spoke, Jake had been rooting through one of the low cupboards. Now he straightened up, holding an empty plastic bottle with a handle moulded into one side. He filled it with water and handed it to Liam. 'Drinking water,' he said.

Liam took it. 'Thanks,' he said.

'Listen, kid,' said Jake. 'Steer clear of this lot. Don't try to talk to them. Do you understand? Talk to any one of them and the freaks'll be after you. They know every-thing that happens in this place. You're lucky you didn't come up to the house. The principal's people would have been on to you in seconds. I finish at four. You got a watch? They won't think anything if I ride home on the bridleway, so I can meet you up at Meregate, okay? You should be able to keep out of view up there.'

Liam hid out for the afternoon in the pines near where he had grounded the punt. He didn't see another person in all that time, which was just as well. Despite the water, the headache and dizziness were getting steadily worse. He wouldn't have had much chance of evading anyone.

Sometime in the middle of the afternoon, he staggered to his feet and followed a path along the creek, heading north. Meregate. That was where Jake had said.

He was almost certainly walking into a trap. But there was just a small chance that Jake would turn out to be on his side.

Meregate was up at the northern boundary of the school, where the manor wall still stood. Inside the wall there were more pine and birch trees and, just beyond, the bridleway ran from the road to the inner shore of the Mere. The gateway was in the north-east corner of the wall.

Liam reached the opening shortly before four. He went to sit in the pines by the Mere. He could see through the trees to Wolsey from here. So close across the water, yet still a two-hour walk. He wondered if Jake would give him a ride again. He would ask, although he didn't know what he would do when he reached town. At least it would be further away from here.

He heard the tinny roar of a motorbike, and then he saw it approaching along the bridleway. A single figure, wearing dark leathers and helmet, on a black bike. It looked like Jake, and he appeared to be alone.

Liam felt another attack of dizziness.

When he looked again, Jake was sitting on his bike, the engine cut out, balancing with his feet on the ground. He had taken his helmet off and was looking around.

Liam tried to get to his feet, but instead stumbled forward on to his hands and knees.

He waited for the world to stop spinning, and then suddenly there were boots in the corner of his vision, a hand on his back.

'You okay, kid? Here, sit back, back against this tree.'

Liam allowed himself to be guided into a sitting position.

Jake was squatting beside him, staring at him. 'Looks like it's taken you bad, doesn't it? Can you hear me, kid?'

'What . . .?' gasped Liam. *What* had taken him bad?

Jake had reached into his jacket pocket, and now he held his hand out flat before Liam. There was a small white pill on it.

'Hnnh?'

'Take it. Go on,' said Jake.

Liam looked at the pill and then at Jake.

'I nicked it,' said Jake. 'Thought you might need it. It's what you Talents take, isn't it? It's what's good for your kind.'

8

In Too Deep

It's true, as they say, that the customer is always right. But it's even truer that the supplier is always in control . . .

Liam took the pill between thumb and forefinger. It seemed familiar, but he couldn't quite place it.

'Go on,' said Jake.

Liam opened his mouth and placed the pill on his tongue. It started to dissolve in his saliva immediately. He knew that taste, that sensation. His stomach groaned violently.

Jake nodded. 'That's right, mate. Normally, they put 'em in your food.'

Liam swallowed, and immediately his head began to clear. After only a few seconds, the dizziness had receded and the pounding ache in his head had eased. 'What is that?' he gasped.

He knew why the pill was familiar now. It looked just like the ones Kath had taken that night to calm herself, that night when she couldn't bear to be with him.

'Control,' said Jake. 'They use 'em to control you. Ain't you ever noticed how freaky that place is? How perfect everything is? How smooth everything runs? No, I don't suppose you would. They use this stuff to control you. But you're hooked. You can't go without it, kid. That's why you got like that. You can't just come off it.'

'How . . . how long do they last?'

'Oh, a day or two,' said Jake. 'I could only nick one tonight, but don't worry. I'll be able to get hold of some more tomorrow.'

Liam looked at him. His thoughts were starting to come more clearly now, and he realized that he was totally dependent on Jake.

'You're hungry, right?' Jake reached up to remove a small backpack he had been wearing. He opened it, found a bread roll and tossed it to Liam.

Liam tore into it immediately. While he did so, Jake produced a big lump of Cheddar and a chicken drumstick from his bag and handed them over.

Eventually, Liam sat back. 'Thank you,' he said.

'No problem,' said Jake. 'Someone helped me once, when I was in the same kind of bother. You should always pass favours on.' He took more bread and cheese from his bag and passed them to Liam. 'So,' he said conversationally, 'what's *your* talent, then?'

Liam looked at him blankly.

'What is it that you can do that none of the rest can?'

Liam shrugged.

'I expect you'll find out soon enough,' said Jake. 'I expect we all will. They seem to think you're important enough . . .'

'What –?'

Jake cut him off with a hand gesture. 'Not now, okay? I've got to get on. Don't want to make 'em suspicious, do we? You never know when they're watching. You got somewhere to hide out? No, don't tell me. I don't want to know where. I'll be back here tomorrow, same time, okay?'

Liam nodded. He didn't know what Jake was up to. Should he trust him?

Jake turned, then hesitated. He took a notebook and pen from his jacket and scribbled something. He handed the note to Liam.

'That's my mobile, okay? Don't call it unless you have to. And that's a friend of mine. He can help with the medication thing. He's cool. You can trust him.'

Liam looked at the note. Below Jake's mobile number there was a name, *Alastair*, and an address: *3 The Coastguards, Wolsey*. When he looked up, Jake was most of the way back to his bike. A short time later, he was off along the bridleway, heading north up past the Mere.

Liam rowed back across the creek to the Point. Now that he had his head straight, he realized that this could not go on for much longer. Eventually someone would spot him, or notice that their boat was missing. He couldn't hide out here indefinitely, living off Jake's handouts.

But the pill changed everything. How could he leave if he was hooked on whatever magic ingredient the pill contained?

Kath . . . She had them. He could go there.

And that was when he made the connection. Not only did Kath have the pills, she must have been feeding them to Liam. He remembered the takeaway, the 'extras' she had fried up to accompany it. And the hearty breakfasts that she prepared for him while she only had toast.

Did this mean that she was a part of whatever was going on? Kath had been all that he had left, but had he ever really had her as an ally at all?

The punt ran aground against the shingle bank of Wolsey Point.

He climbed out and hauled it up above the line of seaweed and driftwood that marked high tide.

He had thought some of Kath's behaviour might have been caused by guilt at her relationship with their parents. Maybe it was guilt of a different order. Guilt about how she was deceiving *Liam* . . .

He found the concrete road again. It had been cast in square slabs, about three metres to each side, and over time they had settled in the shingle so that there were gaps between them, and some blocks were higher than others. Plants grew from the gaps, although there were none where the tyres of the Trust's vehicles must pass.

He came to the single wire strand and ducked under it.

Back in the building where he had spent the night, he stashed the food in a corner, making sure that the bread was covered in its bag in case an enterprising gull came down through the gap in the roof, scavenging.

He had a whole evening ahead. He was tempted to explore. The 'Danger' signs were probably only there for show: a measure to keep local kids out. But the sign warning about unexploded ordnance was worrying. He didn't want to step on a landmine or an unexploded wartime shell.

But if he stuck to the road . . .

He walked. Slowly, he came to understand how

deceptive this landscape of shingle and sand and clay was. He had thought it was pretty much flat, but instead, the wind and sea had carved it into a series of banks and valleys, some quite deep, with precipitous slopes. Nestled in some of these hollows were more ruined buildings. The camp must have been an enormous operation when it had still been in use. There was a complete, deserted town here.

He didn't walk far. Another chain-link fence cut across the Point, with a high gate across the road. A battered old sign read: 'This is a prohibited place. Unauthorized persons entering this area may be arrested and prosecuted.' Another repeated the warning about unexploded ordnance.

He looked through the fence, but couldn't see beyond the next shingle bank, lined with gorse and tamarisk.

There were all kinds of rumours about what type of research had taken place here at Wolsey Camp before it had been closed down. Maybe they had been working on chemical bombs or something, and now all that was left was an area of contaminated ground . . .

Liam turned back.

The gull woke him again the next morning after another unsettled night. This time it wasn't the fevers and pains of withdrawal from the NATS pills that disturbed his sleep, but the sheer cold. He had curled up in the ruined building with only his fleece to warm him. He lay on the heaped sand at one end of the main room, and it cut out some of the chill of the building's concrete floor. But still, it was cold.

In the morning, the gull screeched, and Liam looked up at the blue sky through the gaps in the roof, bleary-eyed and with pains and stiffness in every joint in his body.

He struggled to his feet and made himself do a few awkward stretching exercises.

He took what was left of the food and water down to the mossy shelf by the creek and sat in the shelter of a tamarisk bush. He had caught the sun yesterday and now his forehead and nose were raw with sunburn.

The tide was high again and he saw that the water was lapping at the rear of the punt, where he had dragged it up the bank.

Out in the channel he spotted a small clump of dark seaweed, swirling in the current.

He broke the remaining bread in half and started to chew on one piece. It was hard and had that dry sweetness of old bread. The cheese had dried out too, and he decided to eat all of it now, rather than keeping any for later in the day. He washed it down with what was left of the drinking water.

He felt a sense of calm this morning. It was the first time in days he had felt like this.

He knew a large part of that must be down to the pill he had taken yesterday afternoon. But a part of it was a sense of control that had come to him this morning.

He took a pebble and lobbed it towards the bobbing clump of seaweed out in the creek.

He had decided to confront Jake this afternoon. Jake knew about the pills and he had talked about 'freakish' things at NATS. He must see a lot of what went on there. He clearly knew more than he had let slip.

And after that? Liam only had a couple of pounds, not enough for a rail ticket. But he would head for

Norwich somehow and have it out with Kath.

Between his sister and Jake, Liam was bound to learn something about what had been happening.

The distant sound of the school bell brought him back to the present. Morning call. Time to get up and shower. Back in their room, Anders would be dragging it out for as long as he could, skipping the showers and throwing his clothes on at the last possible minute before breakfast bell. He hoped Anders was looking after Skiver.

Liam remembered grumbling sessions with Anders and Hayley about how NATS took control of everything you did, how everything was timetabled from dawn till night. All they had wanted was a bit of freedom.

He looked around, thinking of the others tumbling into the showers. Now he wasn't bound by the rules and timetable but was he any more free than his friends?

The clump of weed caught Liam's eye again and he looked more closely.

The strands were very fine and dark, maybe ten centimetres long. He had thought at first that they must be growing from the top of a post, or something similar, but now he saw that couldn't be the case. They bobbed about too much, swinging from side to side in the current as the tide fell.

He spotted two black and white ducks then, with red beaks and chestnut bands on their sides. Geese, maybe, rather than ducks. They drifted down the creek, hugging the far bank and eyeing him cautiously. He realized he didn't know much about the natural history of this area. He knew a few of the trees and bushes, but only because Anders had told him their names. He was a city boy at heart. He was out of his depth here.

Now that he had decided to head back to Norwich, he could hardly wait to get moving.

The seaweed . . . it wasn't seaweed.

Now that the tide had edged a little lower, Liam saw that the weed was attached to something pale, something not quite white. Something that swung lazily with the flow of water.

Liam was transfixed.

Time seemed to stretch out around him.

He watched the thing, drifting left, then right, then left again, the dark 'weed' trailing out downstream.

It was a head.

A body. Its feet anchored – weighed down? – in the mud in the centre of the creek.

The dark mass he had taken for fine seaweed was hair.

Liam couldn't take his eyes off the head. It moved with the current in a limp, lifeless way, like a kite in the wind, like a flag on a pole. Like a body with its feet weighed down in a tidal creek.

Just then, the current caught the body, swinging it round towards Liam. The head lolled, turned as if to greet him, and he saw the eyes, the nose, part of the mouth, all set in bloated pale features.

It was Jake.

Liam dragged his gaze away with an enormous effort. He turned and threw up on the shingle and parched moss.

He wiped his mouth on his cuff and looked again.

Jake's head had turned away, but Liam could have sworn the dead face had been smiling at him.

9

The Families

If Liam was truly paranoid, he would think that this was some kind of message. But who would write their messages in blood? Who would allow a human life to be wasted in such a way, simply to get a point across?

Liam did, of course, have every reason to be feeling paranoid by now.

Jake's head lolled sideways again. It was as if he was looking at Liam. Accusing him.

For all that had happened so far, Liam finally had a sense of how serious all this was. Lives were at stake.

At least one life had been lost.

Why? Just for helping Liam?

He thought of his parents then. Their disappearance. Their 'erasure' as that Scottish investigator had put it. Just how complete a thing *was* erasure?

And Kath . . . She was wrapped up in all this, more deeply than he had first realized. Was she okay? Reflexively, he reached for his phone, then stopped himself, remembering that there was no signal out here.

Drifting over on the breeze, he heard the NATS breakfast bell ringing out.

He looked around, then studied the far bank of the creek closely, looking for people among the trees, cameras even. Did they know he was here? Had they known he was here all along, and had they simply been toying with him?

He saw nothing, but that meant little. There was only ever one clear answer in this line of thinking: if you find evidence that the world is against you, then you know you're right; if you find none, then that simply leaves your fears unconfirmed . . .

Out in the channel, Jake drifted. His arms weren't floating. Liam guessed they must be tied together, probably behind his body. That would stop them rising to the surface.

Liam moved towards the boat. He pushed it back into the creek, stepping in as it floated free of the shingle. He was getting quite good at this now. He located the oars in the rowlocks and rowed right-handed until the boat had turned to head upcreek. Putting his body into the effort, he started to row against the tide.

The punt edged out into the channel where the current grew stronger. He wasn't making headway, struggling even to stand still and not float out towards the sea.

Liam had his back to the current and was looking down the punt towards the curve of the creek where it would eventually join the sea. To his horror, he realized that not only was he failing to hold the punt against the current, he was drifting downcreek.

Towards Jake . . .

He rowed hard and managed to slow the boat a little.

If it kept on like this, he would go right over his one-time ally's body. He squeezed his eyes shut. Involuntarily, in his head, he heard the soft clunk that Jake's head would make as it bounced off the flat bottom of the punt.

He opened his eyes and Jake stared back at him, only a couple of metres from the stern of the vessel.

Stop smiling.

Why did he have that smile on his face? The skin had bloated in the seawater. Maybe that was what had pulled his face into that sickly grin.

Liam leaned back and hauled on the oars, over and over again. Eyes closed, he expected the first soft *thunk* of bone on wood at any moment.

When he opened his eyes again, Jake's head was a distant, dark blob on the water.

He didn't dare ease up.

Eventually, the rowing started to come more easily as the creek opened out into a wider, shallower channel. It was just as well that it was easier, as Liam's body protested with every stroke.

He didn't realize he was clear until he saw the fence to his left, extending down into the water. He had passed the fence. He had reached the Mere. He allowed his left arm to rest, and rowed with his right, turning the punt towards the inner shore of the top part of Wolsey Point.

When he could, he stepped out on to a springy mat of salt-marsh vegetation. He turned to face the punt and pushed it away with one foot. He would need it no more. He watched it drift into the channel, and then, moments later, come to rest against the fence.

He staggered across a narrow strip of salt marsh, the springy mat of plants soon giving way to grass and a mixture of sand and shingle. He dropped to his knees and then twisted to sit. He needed to get his breath back. Needed to get his head together. Needed to work out what came next.

He stared at the scrap of paper Jake had given him. Below Jake's mobile number it read, '3 The Coastguards, Wolsey'. That was the address of Jake's friend Alastair. 'He can help with the medication thing,' Jake had said. 'You can trust him.'

Liam would never trust anybody again. But he had judged it worth taking a chance on Jake. Maybe he could take a chance on this Alastair too.

He stood, then went across to the concrete road that ran along from the Point to Wolsey. He saw the high gate in the fence, this time from the northward side. There were several notices on the gate, all battered and worn by exposure to the sea winds.

'Wolsey Camp. Conservation Area. Please respect the wildlife. Keep out. Wolsey Point Preservation Trust.'

'Danger. Unexploded ordnance.'

'This is a prohibited place. Unauthorized persons entering this area may be arrested and prosecuted.'

He turned. To his left was the Mere, now about half water and half exposed mud, dotted with birds. To his right was the steely grey North Sea. Ahead of him, about half a mile away, were the first houses of Wolsey, a terrace of three white coastguards' cottages.

He wondered now at the address. Such a prominent position, with a view of the town, the Point, the marina where Principal Willoughby kept his yacht, and even across the Mere to the rooftops of NATS. A good place from

which to keep an eye on everything. Jake and his friend
. . . had they been watching NATS? Had Jake's help been
less innocent than it had appeared?

Liam walked. The effort was almost too much for him.
His body ached from the rowing and from the nights
sleeping rough. His head throbbed, and he knew it was
the pain of withdrawal, the chemical hook they had sunk
into his body at NATS.

The concrete road became a tarmac-surfaced road by
the cluster of wooden buildings of the sailing club. Either
it was turning into a hot day or Liam was becoming
feverish again. He loosened his shirt. He had left his fleece
back on the Point in his haste to leave. Steadily, he was
losing everything that had ever been his.

The road curved round in front of the cottages. The
row stood at an angle to the beach, looking south-east
over the sea. The first was marked with a number '3'. Liam
approached it and knocked.

The door was opened by a man in jeans and a baggy
brown jumper. He had black-framed glasses and short grey
hair, thinning on top. He smiled and said, 'Liam. I had so
hoped that you would drop by.'

He spoke with a gentle Scottish accent. 'I'm Alastair,'
he continued. 'Do come in.'

Jake's friend was the investigator from Special Intelligence
who had called on Kath with the two Mr Smiths.

Liam sat in the kitchen, a long, narrow room with a wooden
ceiling. On the table in front of him there was a mug of
steaming hot chocolate, fresh from the microwave.

Alastair leaned in the doorway, waiting for Liam to talk.

'Jake said . . .' Liam started, but stopped again. Jake hadn't said much at all.

'Jake's a bit of a wild card,' said Alastair. 'But he's a good operative.'

'He's dead,' said Liam.

Silence.

Finally, Alastair shook his head. 'Damn,' he said softly. 'Where? When?'

'He's in the creek. Near the Camp.' Words. They simplified so much. They didn't come close to describing what Liam had seen. A life snuffed out.

'I told the boy not to take stupid risks,' Alastair continued. 'The stakes are too high.'

Liam stared at him. 'Who are you?' he said. With even the slightest movement, his head spun. His throat was thick, tight, and he found it hard to form words. 'What is this "Special Intelligence" you said you work for? What are you?'

'Take it easy, lad.' Liam felt Alastair's words in his head more than he heard them. He felt them as a reassuring weight. 'It's just like Jake told you. I'm a friend. I'm here to help.'

Liam swallowed. 'Jake . . . He said you would help.' He stopped, started again. 'The medication,' he said. 'Jake said you could help with the medication.'

They were in a room. Not the kitchen, but still in the cottage, Liam thought. He could see heaped gravel outside the window.

He felt dizzy.

He leaned on his elbows on a pine dining table, his head in his hands. He could feel the pulse from his temples drumming in his palms like a captured moth.

Alastair was there, and Mr Smith. The first Mr Smith, that is. The one who had answered Kath's door, not the one in the car. Maybe that meant he was the second Mr Smith, then.

Whichever, Mr Smith stood by the window, arms folded, watching as Alastair sat down opposite Liam and opened an attaché case. It looked like a doctor's case, or that of a travelling pharmaceutical salesman. Jars and bottles and syringes nestled among dividers, some retained by black elasticated straps.

Alastair took out one unmarked white plastic pot, then another, and another.

With a thumb, he flipped open the lid of each and looked inside.

'Well,' he said. 'Which to give you?' He pushed the three pots towards Liam with the side of his hand. 'We have white ones, pink ones, blue ones . . . Pills to shut it out. Pills to let it in. Some to make it stronger and some to kill it off. What's your fancy, Liam? Which one should we give you?'

Liam looked at the pots and then at Alastair. The man seemed to be enjoying himself.

'"It",' said Liam. 'What's "*it*"?'

Alastair smiled. 'Oh, Liam,' he said. 'You really don't know, do you?' He took a single white pill from the nearest pot and slid it across the table towards Liam. 'Take this,' he said. 'I'm pretty sure this is what they've been giving you. They like to keep us under control.'

Us . . .

Liam stared at the tablet, and for a moment he wondered what would happen if he refused it, if he tried to see out these withdrawal symptoms. Then he reached for it, took it between forefinger and thumb and placed it on his tongue.

It dissolved instantly.

'You and me, Liam. Mr Smith too. We're not like the others. We're different. We're . . . *more* than them.'

Liam stared at him. It was the oddest sensation. As the pill started to take effect his head was clearing and yet . . . yet everything seemed to be getting weirder and weirder.

'What are you saying?'

Alastair leaned back, pushing his glasses up over the bridge of his nose with an index finger. 'Have you never noticed anything odd about your world? Anything strange?'

Liam shrugged. 'How would I know?' he said. His world, his family and friends, the things they did and said – they were what he knew, so of course they were what he thought of as normal.

Alastair sighed. 'They really have managed to shelter you, haven't they?' He paused, then went on. 'This is how we survive. This is how we have survived centuries of persecution. We hide our true nature from the world, even from our own children.'

'What "true nature"?' Liam's head was clear now. Too clear, maybe.

'Like I say, lad, we're different. You, me, Mr Smith, half the kids at the academy . . . we're members of the Lost Families. We're not human, Liam. Or at least, we're a different kind of human. A gifted kind.'

Liam stared at him. He was in the company of a madman. Two madmen.

'Oh, I know what you're thinking, Liam. You think we're mad.'

Liam opened his mouth to deny it, but was cut off by Alastair's next words.

'That wasn't a random choice of phrase, Liam. I *know* what you're thinking. Not word by word, not the intimate, embarrassing detail. But your thoughts have shape and I can reach out and grasp those shapes and make sense of some of them. I can *push* them too.'

Instantly, Liam flashed back to their first encounter in Kath's flat. Or was the memory triggered, pulled out by some other force? He remembered the urge to tell Alastair everything. That urge had come from nowhere, it seemed. Or had it come from outside?

Back in the cottage . . . Alastair watched him intently.

'You don't believe me, of course,' he said. 'About seventy-five per cent of you doesn't believe me. But the remaining twenty-five per cent is entertaining the possibility that I might be the first person to tell you the truth about who you are, who *we* are. Give it time, Liam: that twenty-five per cent will expand. You will come to believe me. And then you'll start to make sense of what's been happening.'

'You mean you read minds,' muttered Liam.

'And control them, or push them a little,' said Alastair. 'It's only a moderate talent, but it's my most developed one. Have you never felt the world pressing in on you, Liam? Have you never sensed what's going on in the heads

94

of those around you? Or has it always been kept under control?'

Liam shrugged. Of course he'd felt that. *Every*one felt that. Didn't they? 'What do you mean, about the Lost Families?'

'We've suffered,' said Alastair. 'Our kind have always suffered. We have a range of talents, what they call psi powers: mind-reading and control, grasping the shape of future events, even affecting physical objects at a distance. Sometimes in the past our kind have been held up as religious visionaries and leaders. More often, we've been persecuted for witchcraft or anything else they can pin on us. It's only in the last century or two that we've re-emerged and got together with others of our own kind. Before then, we were almost driven out of existence. Now, the Families have reunited and we have networks all around the world. You'd be surprised how many very important people are actually members of the Lost Families. People in power.'

'NATS . . .?'

'We educate our own. The Talented and Special.'

'But I'm just a Grunt,' said Liam. He had a place at NATS because his father worked for the ministry, not because he had been singled out as particularly talented in any respect.

'Sometimes the greatest talents are late to emerge. They can be buried deep within the mind. It's a protective mechanism.'

'Protection?' said Liam. What was he implying? 'Protect me from what?'

'No,' said Alastair. 'You misunderstand. Not to protect *you* – to protect the rest of *us*.'

10

Home Again

It was like learning that red is blue and up is really down.

The world is not the world, Liam: the world is different. You are different to other people. They are the family of humankind, but we are something *else*.

Sometime around the middle of the day, they ate fish and chips that Mr Smith brought back from the town.

Liam had sat quietly in the front room for a time. Alastair had left him in peace, giving him space to think.

About a world where humankind was divided between normal humans and *others*.

About the Lost Families.

About people with strange powers strategically placed throughout society – leaders, people of influence, people who made a difference.

About how everything had to be seen differently, re-interpreted in the light of this hidden power struggle. Was that why all this was happening? Had he and his parents become some kind of threat to the big secret of the Families?

And about being different. Did he have these gifts? All he

wanted was to get back to a normal, quiet life, but that had been ripped away from him forever if any of this was true.

The banging of doors and the smell of chips led him through to the kitchen again. Alastair and Mr Smith were seated at the narrow table, unwrapping the takeaway.

'Oh, not salt and vinegar!' Alastair complained. 'I told you: no salt and vinegar.' He turned to Liam and said, 'If I want salt and vinegar I can add my own. Don't you find that the most annoying thing?'

Liam sat at the vacant seat and took a chip. 'What's happening?' he said in the kind of firm, quiet voice that cuts through any background noise. 'What happened to my parents? What's happening to me? What have they been doing to me and my friends at NATS?'

Alastair broke open a piece of fish, so that its white flesh was exposed.

'Your parents . . .' he said. 'We're puzzled about that too. We're still looking into it, but I'll admit that we're not making much progress. The Families have their disagreements. There are different factions, different groups, each with their own agenda. Me and the Mr Smiths stand back from it all: Special Intelligence mediates between the government and the Lost Families, preventing any extreme courses of action. The government have a lot at stake with us. They want our kind to work with them – *for* them. And they can't let us get out of control. Our kind of person can be dangerous, you know. We need watching.' He gave a grunt of laughter. 'I think that either one or both of your parents turned against the Families, Liam. Or against Willoughby, at least. I don't know the detail. I

97

don't know the reason. It may have been simply a case of money talking, or they may have some ideological grudge. As you can imagine, there are some strange ideas about.

'Whatever. One or both of them went too far, and my guess is that the Families have reacted by making them non-persons, removing any trace that they have existed.'

Erasing them.

'But what happened to them?'

Alastair shrugged and straightened his glasses again. 'If they're lucky, they will have been taken in hand and re-educated. Our kind are good at that. We're good at manipulating people's minds.'

He didn't elaborate on what might have happened if they had been unlucky.

'Will I ever see them again?'

'Probably not, lad,' said Alastair. 'You have to hope for the best, but even in the very best outcome you're not likely to be reunited. I'm sorry.'

Liam took a chip and toyed with it between forefinger and thumb. He had no appetite.

He wanted to strike out. He wanted to find out what special talent he had, if any, and turn it on the people who felt that it was right to reach into his life and chew it over like this. He wanted to hurt someone.

'Anger's understandable,' said Alastair. 'But it's not going to get you anywhere.'

He felt a calming pressure in his mind and he tried to imagine himself pushing it away. He didn't want this calm and reasonable madman exerting any kind of influence on him. He clung on to his anger.

'Okay,' said Alastair. 'Okay.'

A long silence descended. Outside, it started to rain and Liam watched the water tracking down the window, channels running, joining, combining into a huge network across the glass.

'There was a time when we thought Katherine was something rather special, you know.'

Liam looked at Alastair. How did this man know his sister so well?

'I taught her at the academy. We have people there, observers. Jake was one. I was another for a time. Some of their practices are . . . a bit extreme, shall we say. They need watching. Sometimes we work with them, sometimes we have to pull them back into line. I spent five years there.'

'Kath?'

'We thought she was going to be a star student. She was fast-tracked almost as soon as she arrived. But something in her tests flagged her up as one to watch for other reasons: danger signals.'

'What do you mean, "danger signals"?' Liam hadn't known Kath had done well at NATS, even if only briefly. He only knew that she had gone for two terms and then been dropped. He had been young then and the memories were all vague.

'She couldn't hack it. Couldn't take the pace. It's all one big filtering process, you see. Even before the academy. The national curriculum and SATS? All those tests every schoolchild has to sit every couple of years or so? Whatever reason they give publicly, the real reason for all that is to identify children of talent. The Families have hidden themselves so well over the generations that many of our kind don't even know that they belong. We are scattered through the so-called normal world. We have to do what we can to identify our own kind and return them to the fold.

'It's hard to be sure, though. When a child is identified with possible talent, he or she must be taken aside for more testing. That's what schools like NATS do. They provide an environment where we can test and filter those who might be descended from the Lost Families. Over time, pupils are sorted into those who may be ignored, then those of our own kind, and those who may be a threat. The first are filtered out. The second get inducted into the Families in Senior House.'

'And the third?'

'It depends on the nature of the threat. Remember that the Families have been persecuted for centuries. We cannot allow rogue talents to threaten our survival. Katherine was identified in the third category, Liam. She was an extreme sensitive. The world talked to her. Sometimes it shouted at her. Her talent couldn't be controlled, so she was treated. They operated on her to kill off the sensitive parts of her brain. They sterilized her so that there was no danger of her rogue talent being inherited by future generations. The operation on her brain was not entirely successful. She will be on medication for the rest of her life. I don't expect you to be grateful, Liam, but that was my doing, giving her that chance: there were others who wanted to remove her from the picture altogether . . .'

Liam stared at the rain tracks on the window. He

remembered being with Kath in Norwich and realizing how little he knew her. He remembered how sensitive she was to his presence, how she couldn't bear to have him close.

'You, Liam,' Alastair continued. 'You're definitely not in the first category. The Families are not going to ignore you.'

Liam felt like the victim of some almighty hoax. The biggest practical joke in the world, at his expense. How could he believe such impossible things?

But he had known that Kath was a woman who nursed deep wounds, and this was the first time he had been given any kind of explanation.

Still he fought against believing what Alastair had told him. If he accepted it, then he was accepting the likelihood that he would never see his parents again, that he would never even know what had happened to them.

He couldn't give up on them so easily.

Alone again in the front room, he took out his phone and flipped it open. He watched as it went through its powering-up routine: battery okay, PIN code. He thumbed the number in and waited to see if there were any messages. The signal here was weak but better than none.

Then a message he had not seen before appeared on the screen. 'User not recognized. Please call our network sales team to register this mobile.'

He stared at it. His account was in credit, his PIN was the same as it had always been, so why wasn't it recognizing him?

Just then, Alastair came in and tossed Liam a can of Coke.

'What's up?' he asked, seeing the look on Liam's face.

Liam turned his phone to Alastair. 'It's not recognizing me,' he said. 'My account's dead . . .'

'Do you have any other means of contacting the world? Email? IRC?'

Liam nodded. 'Email,' he said.

'Come with me.'

Liam followed his host through the house to the dining room again. Alastair's notebook PC was plugged into the wall. Alastair stooped to do something, and a few seconds later Liam heard the tone dialling and then the whine and crackle of a modem shaking hands with the world.

'There,' said Alastair. 'All yours.'

Liam sat at the table and looked at the desktop icons. He found Internet Explorer and started it up, then typed the URL of his webmail service.

'Welcome, guest,' it told him. 'New user? <u>Register now.</u> Existing user: type username _____ password _____. <u>Lost your password?</u>'

He typed his username, *liamconnor34*, and his password, *c4n4rIes*.

'INVALID ENTRY,' it told him. 'USER NOT KNOWN. New user? <u>Register now.</u>'

He tried again, with the same result.

Alastair had been watching over his shoulder. He put a hand gently on Liam's back. 'Well,' he said. 'It looks like you've been erased too, lad.'

Liam stood at the window, watching the rain.

'This could be their biggest mistake,' said Alastair, from

the table. He had been tapping away on his notebook computer, but now he snapped it shut and sat back with his hands interlocked behind his head. 'I've just checked a few directories and databases I can get into. There's no trace of you, Liam. No trace of you or your parents. You're a non-person. No background, no ties. You're nobody. You're nameless. Your only current existence is here, in number three The Coastguards, Wolsey, Suffolk. You could be anyone you want to now. We could create a new identity for you. We're good at that. I've been two other people, myself.'

Liam said nothing.

They were offering him freedom. A blank page.

But it would mean accepting all the losses. Saying goodbye forever to any chance of seeing his parents again, to Kath and to his friends stuck at NATS. It would mean drawing a line under them all.

This man was offering him normality and Liam realized that he did not want that any more. He could not accept it, after glimpsing the depths that lay behind what was, for most people, the normal, everyday world.

And there was the small matter of the little white pills. These people would always have a hold over him.

Normality . . . freedom . . . they were all an illusion. A gift offered, only to be snatched away when the puppet-master decreed. He would never be free if he accepted gifts like this. The only real freedom was that which he could create for himself.

He turned to face Alastair.

'No,' he said. 'I want to do things on my own terms now. I'm fed up with being pushed around. Can I borrow your phone? I want to talk to my sister.'

'That's a very bold decision, lad,' said Alastair. 'Most people, having seen what you have, would run a mile.' He reached into his trouser pocket and produced a mobile. He opened it and slid it across the table towards Liam. 'You'll find her number under "K" for Katherine.'

In the front room again, Liam studied Alastair's mobile. He found the phonebook, then found Katherine's number. **Call?** it asked him. He pressed the 'okay' button and listened to the tones as it dialled.

What to say?

He understood. That would be enough.

He understood and he wanted to come up to Norwich and talk.

Whatever. They had to learn to talk to each other some-time, and that time might as well be now.

The phone was picked up on the third ring. A man's voice answered. 'Hello?' it said. 'Who's that?'

For an instant, Liam thought Alastair must have the wrong number for Kath stored in his phone. 'Erm, it's me,' he said. 'Liam. I was –'

'Liam! Are you okay? Where are you? Listen, Liam, are you okay?'

It was his father.

Liam realized he had taken the phone away from his ear and was just staring at it in amazement.

'Liam. Are you still there?'

'Dad . . . What happened? Where's Mum? Are you with Kath?'

'I'm okay, Liam. We're all okay. Listen, can you get here? Where are you? I can't talk now. Come to Kath's place, okay? Will you do that, Liam?'

'I'll get there, Dad.'

'Good, good. Hang on in there, Liam. Things aren't always what they appear, but we'll get through all this together, okay? Can you make it this afternoon?'

'I'll be there.'

'You want to go to Norwich?'

Liam nodded, fighting hard to control his thoughts. 'I know you've helped me a lot already and I don't have any right to ask for more. But I don't have enough money for the train. And . . . I need the medication.'

Alastair studied him closely. 'What if Katherine doesn't want to talk to you?'

'I'll handle that if I have to,' said Liam. He had said nothing about the conversation with his father, clamping down on any thought of this as soon as it arose. They didn't need to know.

'You're a one for bold decisions, aren't you?'

Alastair opened his attaché case and took out a plastic pot. He thumbed the lid open and tipped it, with a finger over the opening to control the flow of tablets. He tipped out seven pills on to the tabletop. 'A week's worth,' he said. He took a small brown envelope and a pen from a pocket in the lid of the case and wrote down a phone number. 'One a day,' he said. 'They deaden your sensitivities. NATS only want any talents to emerge in a closely controlled environment. Don't be tempted to take more if things get tough. And don't try to get yourself off them – you're well and truly hooked. That's one of the ways they control us. That's my phone number. I want you to phone me before you run out. I want to know where you get to and I want to be able to extract you if you get into trouble. Do you understand?'

Liam nodded. He had a week.

Alastair took out a wallet, licked a finger and peeled off five twenties. 'Enough?' he said. 'That should cover your train and anything else you run into. If not, call. Okay?'

Liam nodded. 'Thanks,' he said. He meant it. Whatever Alastair was up to, here in this cottage on the beach, he had just bought Liam's passage back to his family.

'A word of advice, lad. There are no bystanders in this game. None. Everyone is either a player or a victim.'

Liam nodded. 'I think I'd just about realized that,' he said.

He was back in Norwich by mid-afternoon. All the time on the train he had studied his fellow passengers. Were any of them players, or were they all victims, trapped in an illusion of normality?

He was excited, he realized.

He was astounded to think how many upheavals and awful shocks he had been through in the last few days.

And here he was, riding the train home. On his way to see Dad and, he hoped, Mum. And his big sister, with whom he now had some kind of deep connection. He felt like a little boy again.

He looked a mess, he knew. He'd had a wash at 3 The

Coastguards, but he still looked like someone who had been sleeping rough.

The taxi driver gave him a funny look, but he didn't grumble when Liam waved a twenty-pound note and gave him Kath's address. They stopped and started through the city traffic and Liam grew impatient. He wanted to be *there*.

He paid the driver and went over to Kath's front door, peering up at the first-floor window in case they were there, looking down.

A folded-over note was pinned to the wood:

Liam.
Working till 5 @ KidActive round the corner.
See you there?

Liam had noticed the nursery before. He remembered wondering why they always had to have such dumb names.

He knocked on the door. Kath might be out, but it wasn't his sister he'd come to see.

No reply.

He checked the note again, then turned on his heel and strode back down the road.

It was an ordinary detached house, set back from the street, with a long front garden. Some children were playing a ball game on the lawn while a young woman watched. She looked at Liam quizzically.

'I'm Kath's brother,' he said. 'She told me to come and find her here. Is that okay?'

Absently, the woman nodded towards the house. 'They're all inside,' she said.

Just then, the ball rolled past Liam's feet. Instinctively, he trapped it, flipped it up with his toe and side-footed it back to a small blonde girl. She laughed and kicked at it, missing completely.

Liam smiled at her, then walked up the long, straight path to the front door. He felt good. Relaxed.

The door was partly open and he knocked, then pushed at it.

He entered a gloomy corridor. Two rows of coat hooks lined one wall, with tiny coats crowding for space. Excited, high-pitched laughter came through the open door of the room on his right.

Liam stood in the doorway and looked in.

Kath was there, squatting next to a small boy, helping him with his shoe. The boy had a hand in her hair, stroking it like a comfort blanket.

Liam had never seen such a look on his sister's face. This was her element. She was a natural here. Maybe those sensitivities they had never quite managed to kill off gave her a special understanding with these children.

That reminded him of what else Alastair had claimed: that Kath had been sterilized. Stop her breeding. Stop her from extending her bad bloodline. It sounded like some kind of Nazi project from the last century: controlling the breeding of those seen as inferior.

'Okay, then,' said Kath, straightening. 'Who wants to sing another song?'

There was a chorus of enthusiastic children's voices.

She glanced across, just then, and saw Liam. She nodded, then looked away, thrown off her stride. Liam told himself that he shouldn't feel disappointed. It was unreasonable to expect everything to be fine between them the moment he turned up.

'Okay, then,' said Kath to her class. '"London's Burning"? Here we go. Remember your three groups, Lions, Tigers and Leopards? Just the Lions first of all.'

She started them singing.

'London's burning, London's burning . . .'

As the first group moved on to 'Fire! Fire! Fire! Fire!' Kath pointed at a second group and they started with the first line. Liam remembered singing this when he was little. He'd loved this song, loved the battling voices, the clash of words, the way the tunes of the different lines interlocked.

'Pour on water, pour on water.' The third group joined in with the first line as the second sang the second line and the first the third line.

'*And* again . . .'

The cacophony of high-pitched voices scattered around the right tune, singing three different stages of the same song simultaneously, was quite astounding. It was an exciting sound. An exhilarating one.

Liam had to hold on to the door frame, the sensations made him so dizzy, the sounds swirling around his head, holding him, transfixing him.

'Liam! You made it.'

'Dad.' He didn't even have to turn to know that it was his father who had come to stand at his shoulder. 'It's . . .'

'Liam, son. I'm sorry. But this is for your own good.

You're better off in our protection than charging around like a mad thing.'

He turned and saw that his father was not alone. Standing with him was the fake policeman from the house, the one with the thin face, the ever-present fuzz of stubble, the always-moving, twitching eyes. And with him, the other policeman, the one from the station. DC Parker.

Smiling, Parker said, 'We get everywhere, don't we? Our kind.'

Everyone is either a player or a victim.

'And *again* . . .'

The noise filled his head. But something else was there too. A presence. A pressure.

He wanted to run, but that presence would not allow him to move.

He wanted to lash out. He wanted to beat his father with his fists, demand to know why he had betrayed him like this. But the presence smothered him, stopped him from doing anything.

It started to slow down his thoughts too. Snuff them out, one by one, until he was still seeing but everything was just shapes, patterns of light and dark. The shapes weren't even people because his mind was blank, incapable of doing anything with the information his eyes sent to his brain.

And then: blackness.

11

Under the Knife

Fear can be a powerful thing. If something scares you, it will stick in your memory for a long time. If something really scares you, scares you in a life-threatening, serious trauma kind of way, then its lesson will be imprinted on your mind in a far more fundamental way: a subconscious thing, a lesson learned in ways that affect your gut reactions, not mere memories of events.

If something scares you even more than that, then it can start the job of rewiring the person that you are.

Darkness.

Darkness and movement. A shaking, forward motion. Lying on his back, but moving headfirst. Shaking, rattling.

Sound too, then. Rattling and an occasional muffled drone of a voice like a slowed-down tape.

Liam was lying on his back, on some kind of trolley, being wheeled somewhere.

Thoughts struggled through his mind. Slow thoughts, as if each was weighed down, or pushing through mud.

Mud in his head.

The creek. Jake's head, drifting slowly from side to side

in the current. Slow, like Liam's thoughts. Smiling. What was there to smile about?

A distant chorus of young voices. Singing 'London's Burning'. Kath's look. Guilt. Betrayal.

Dad . . .

He opened his eyes.

A circular light on the ceiling above him, moving down towards his feet, then gone. Glimpses of wall to his left, with noticeboards, pieces of paper stuck there with drawing pins and staples. Wood panelling to his right, dark wood with a deep, deep polish. A door, of the same dark wood, then it too was gone.

It looked like one of the corridors in the main NATS building. Why would they have brought him here?

There was a thud and a dragging sound and the trolley slowed sharply. Swing doors. They clattered against the sides of Liam's trolley, then a hand reached forward from somewhere near Liam's feet to push one door away again.

This room was darker, and there were what looked like surgical gowns hanging from hooks on one wall. It smelled like . . . that hospital smell . . .

They went through some more swing doors and stopped. The light was brighter again here. Too bright when you were lying on your back looking up at a bank of harsh lamps above you.

There were more people in this place, several different voices. A hum of machinery.

A man moved into view just then. He was wearing a mint green gown with a cloth mask over the lower part of his face and a white surgical hood tied at the back, covering his greying hair. He glanced at Liam, then turned away, intent on whatever it was that he was doing.

Liam bucked his body, trying to sit up, to get to his feet, to run.

He couldn't.

He was strapped down.

He arched his neck so that he could look down his own body. Two black straps stretched across his chest, with more pinning down his arms and legs.

He was naked. And he was strapped down in an operating theatre. He didn't dare think about what was to come next.

For a long time, none of them seemed particularly interested in him, and he lay there, body rigid, straining at the straps.

A hand came into view from the right, pushing his head back down. Then another strap was passed across his forehead and pulled tight. Someone pushed two cold, hard blocks against his face from either side, so that finally his head was locked in position. The only parts of his body he could move were his eyes, mouth, fingers and toes.

A head loomed over, a hand holding a hypodermic syringe with a long, fine needle.

Through its surgical mask, the face said, 'Hello, Liam. My name's Brian and I'll be your anaesthetist today. Let's deaden things a bit, shall we? I think you'll appreciate that.'

The needle came down, and for an awful moment Liam thought it was going to be stuck in his eye. Instead, it moved past and there was a tiny prickle of pain on his forehead, just about the centre of the hairline. Another to the right, and then to the left. Then more across his scalp. There didn't seem to be any hair in the way of these injections – no sensation of it being pushed aside to make way for the needle – and he realized he had been shaved.

Naked, hairless, unable to move. It felt like everything had been stripped away from him.

'It'll take a few minutes,' said Brian the anaesthetist, looming back into view. 'We should have some music on really, shouldn't we? Something to occupy your mind. You'd probably like that, wouldn't you?' He moved away and Liam could only stare at the lights. Even with his eyes shut, they glared through his eyelids.

They were going to do something . . . to his head.

He could feel the numbness spreading. Before, he had felt the gentle movement of air across his scalp as people moved about, but now there was just a fuzzy warmth, a nothingness.

His head. His brain.

They had operated on Kath. They had killed off the sensitive part of her brain in order to remove her talent. Or they had tried to, at least – Alastair had said it hadn't been a complete success, which was why she was still sensitive.

Were they going to do that to Liam now? Kill off a part of his brain? Erase an aspect of himself that he had never even known existed?

Was this to be the end of all that had been happening? Had they rounded him up just to do this and then dump him back into a so-called normal life, like they had with Kath?

Perhaps that was for the best. He could almost see himself adjusting to things, just as Kath had. Living within whatever limits they imposed on him.

'Feel that?' A face drifted into view. Brian again. 'No, I don't think you did.' He must have done something to test the sensitivity of Liam's scalp. Liam had felt nothing. 'Okay, he's all yours, Sir Peter.'

Brian moved away and another face appeared. Sir Peter, Liam guessed. Then he recognized the sharp, hawk-like features peering at him over the surgical mask. Principal Willoughby! Or rather, Sir Peter Willoughby.

He said nothing. He studied Liam's features closely, and then nodded.

Liam just wanted this to be over. Whatever they were doing. He had no choice, no escape. Let them kill off a part of his brain and make him a dull, ordinary person like almost anyone else.

'No, Connor,' said Willoughby. 'It's not as simple as all that. We could never let you go. Not with your pedigree. You are special. And you are ours.'

Liam stared at him.

'We've been testing you for fifteen years, Connor. You pass every time. You are our star student. You should be proud now, while you're allowed to know this.'

Fifteen years. They'd been monitoring him since he was born . . . If Willoughby was telling the truth. Tests. He remembered Alastair talking about the filtering process, trying to identify descendants of the Lost Families. But how had they known to test him from so early?

'Oh, the filtering is only a part of it, Connor. It's how

we identify the wheat from the chaff, the raw talents who emerge through generations of mixed breeding, lost in the general gene pool. You are not part of that flotsam, though, Connor. Your bloodline is almost pure Families. We know that because we bred you. We chose the egg. We chose the sperm. You are the product of our breeding programme, just as your parents were before you. Others have been . . . damaged . . . but you are still intact. We have high hopes of you, Connor. High hopes indeed.'

Liam closed his eyes, his last line of defence. Why believe this?

'Because it's the truth. Your father knows that. He knows where his loyalties lie.'

Liam opened his eyes. He could hide nothing from this monster!

My father is a cheat. He lied to me. He trapped me. He handed me over to you. I don't care what he thinks, or who he is loyal to. Did he do this to my mother too?

Willoughby smiled, an unexpectedly gentle expression. 'Your father is a good man,' he said. 'And your mother is dead. She died nine years ago.'

No!

Willoughby nodded. 'There's no reason for me to lie to you now, Connor. You won't remember this soon. The memory will be erased. We're good with memories, you see. We have a number of techniques for managing them in our subjects. We can remove them, just like that.' He sliced a hand through the air, back past his head, to demonstrate. 'And we can add them too. We really are very good with them.'

Liam closed his eyes, an act of resignation now rather than defiance.

'Think, Connor. How much can you remember? How much can you *really* remember?'

He thought of his mother. His weekend visit home at the start of the month. They hadn't really done much. Just watched TV and shared the house. She was a stocky woman, a little shorter than average, with the same half-curled mid-brown hair that Kath had. Dark eyes. A narrow mouth with lips that were often pursed, in frustration or amusement or concentration.

He couldn't put it all together, though. Couldn't *picture* her.

But they could be doing this to him now! Muddling his thoughts. Messing with his memories. His mother was real. Had been real. He wouldn't let her go.

Liam watched the surgeon hold her scalpel up to the light, as if inspecting it for flaws.

They were going to keep him awake while . . . while they did whatever it was they were going to do to him.

'Stress is a great educator,' said Willoughby, somewhere off to Liam's right. 'Think of all the stress you have undergone, Liam. The trials, the fears, the threats to your cosy existence . . . all designed to help us shape the person you will become – all designed to help your talent emerge from the recesses of your mind.'

Liam thought, then, of his missing parents, the wrecked house, the time he had spent on the run, Jake . . .

'That's right, Liam. This is a scientific programme. There

is a reason for everything. Intense trauma imprints itself on the human nervous system far more deeply than we can ever reach with the knife. Believe me, we've tried all the alternatives.'

The surgeon's left hand rested lightly on Liam's forehead.

Something happened, higher up towards the crown of his skull. He didn't feel it. He didn't experience any pain, any pressure. But he knew it had happened.

'Only a small incision,' said the surgeon. She had a gentle, kind voice. Some kind of northern accent that Liam couldn't quite place. 'Big enough for the drill. You'll hardly notice it once it's healed.'

Liam stared straight ahead. The lights. The blinding, dazzling lights. They blanked out his vision. Made everything white. Hid any hint of detail. He concentrated on that whiteness harder than he had ever concentrated before.

Somewhere, an electric motor revved, whined. Someone was gunning the drill, as if to taunt him.

'Right now,' said Willoughby, somewhere in the far distance, 'we're working on several levels. On the one hand, a team of talent-operatives is working on your memories: selecting, sorting, reshaping. On the other, Doctor Shastri here is about to implant a device which will allow you to gain control of your powers. It's standard practice for our more valuable assets. It will, of course, allow *us* more complete control over your powers too. This is a team endeavour, and you, no matter how special you may turn out to be, are a mere squad player, Connor. And on another hand, if that were possible, the trauma of the moment is opening you up to us. Your brain is offering itself up to us in surrender, just asking us to reshape it, to blot out what you are experiencing.'

'Come on, Sir Peter,' said Brian, the anaesthetist. 'This isn't the time for one of your speeches. We don't want the anaesthetic to wear off, do we?'

Softly, Willoughby said, 'Perhaps we should. It would intensify the trauma . . .'

Liam tried to shut him out, but there was no escaping his words.

'There's one more thing I want to tell you, Connor.' Willoughby spoke so softly that the words seemed to be just trickling gently into Liam's ears, seeping in. Somehow that made them seem all the more intense.

'One thing that I want to imprint itself deep in your subconscious mind so that you always know it. Like I said, Connor, we have high hopes for you. We think you may be very special indeed. But you may also turn out to be dangerous and we cannot allow that. We are watching you. We are watching you very closely indeed. And if, in our judgement, the risk outweighs the benefits of continuing this experiment, we will call it to a close. Do you understand me? We will eliminate all trace of what has happened. You will never be allowed to pose us a serious threat.'

The whiteness. Dazzling. Liam concentrated on the light and the silence after Willoughby's words.

And then he heard the electric whine again.

He felt the drilling, despite the anaesthetic. There was no pain, but the vibration set his skull ringing, his jaw, his cheekbones, the vertebrae in his neck. The vibration jarred. It made his flesh quiver.

And the noise . . .

Like a dentist's drill, only deeper in pitch, the vibrations slower as the bit ground through skull-bone. And louder. It droned manically in his ears, as if someone was drilling into a stone wall right next to his head.

He closed his eyes and still he saw the white.

He smelled burning. Electrical burning. What was happening? No. More barbecue smoke than electrical. Was it the heat of the drill . . .? No, he realized the sound had stopped. They must have broken through his skull.

'That's right, Connor. You may experience all kinds of strange sensations now. Random firing of the nerves in your brain, now that we have found our way in.'

The smell was apples now. It had always been apples. What had he been thinking of?

'Ooh,' said Dr Shastri, somewhere above him. 'I'd forgotten we were on the fifteen mil – look, I can get my pinky right in!'

Pressure. In his head. A drowning sensation.

Liam gasped for air.

There was a pain behind his forehead. Something pressing on the back of his eye. Moving.

'Wiggle wiggle wiggle!' laughed the surgeon.

What were they doing? He was dreaming, he suddenly realized. He would wake up at home . . . wherever that was.

'This is a very delicate procedure, you know,' said Brian, leaning in close over Liam. 'One slip and whooo! That's you, vegetable of the day. Just as well you're in the hands of professionals, isn't it?'

Home . . . he tried to remember it. Tried to think of the front door, the hall, the colour of the carpets, his bedroom. Gone.

He felt presences in his head, pressures that were not put there by Dr Shastri. Tidying up. Erasing.

He was powerless to resist them. He had been opened up. He had surrendered. Let them do what they will.

He saw Dr Shastri, holding some kind of long, pointed tweezers with a small metallic cube in their grip.

The little finger of one gloved hand was smeared red up to the second knuckle.

She moved out of view again. 'Just pop this in,' she muttered.

'We're almost done,' said Willoughby. 'You've been very cooperative.'

Liam was suddenly angry. He was not going to submit to them so easily!

'And what are you going to do, then?' asked Willoughby. 'You are at our complete mercy.'

He would remember.

He let his eyes close again, more slowly this time, more heavy-lidded.

He thought of Alastair, and the sensation of pushing his presence away. He tried to do that again, tried to picture a barrier between himself and Willoughby.

And then he tried to remember.

The Point. The ruined building. The gull that woke him at first light, peering down through the hole in the roof, throwing its head back to screech its morning greeting. He remembered 3 The Coastguards, the chips, and the realization that no one could give him freedom, he must create it. Hanging out at Three Trunker with Anders and Hayley. His father. The look on his father's face as he had deceived him, trapped him, while the children sang 'London's Burning' in the next room.

He clung on for as long as he could, and then he slipped.

'He's going,' he heard Brian the anaesthetist say. 'He's losing consciousness. I can't bring him back.'

'I know,' said Willoughby. 'I felt him going.' And then he must have leaned closer, because his next words were spoken straight into Liam's right ear. 'Sleep now, Connor. Open your mind to the new you.'

I2

Starting Over

The sun shone, the sky was blue with a few drifts of wispy white. Birds sang from the poplar trees. It was just another normal day, the first Monday in June, the first day of the second half of Summer Term. But for Liam Connor it was to be his first day at the National Academy for the Talented and Special. A new start. A big opportunity, they had told him – not everyone gets through the tough selection procedure to get into NATS.

It was to be the first day of a new life, although Liam didn't understand quite how true that was.

The taxi had dropped him on a semicircular gravelled area before the main building. They had driven up the long poplar-lined drive, and all the time Liam had looked out of the front of the car, staring at the grand building. He had only ever seen places like this on day trips: a stately home, a picnic in the grounds with peacocks strutting around, children laughing and crying. It was hard to believe he was going to be living in such a place.

He felt very lucky.

He thought of the grubby little flat that Aunt Katherine

had in Norwich. Liam had been staying there for the last few weeks while his father was away on business, sorting out some kind of transfer at work. Dad wouldn't tell him what that involved, but then he often couldn't talk about his work. Liam suspected it would mean that his father was going to be away again, travelling. That was the downside to boarding at NATS: he would see much less of his father.

The building had a long frontage, with two rows of leaded windows looking blankly out along the drive. Square towers stood at the front corners of the building, each with a flagpole, bearing on the left the Union flag and on the right the flag of the European Union.

Before him, wide stone steps led up between white columns to a double door, hooked open, welcoming him in.

Liam hauled his big suitcase up the steps, then, at the top, changed grips so that it would run on its castors behind him. Inside, there was a reception desk, behind which sat a sour-faced man. Behind him, there were several ranks of pigeon holes, some stuffed with envelopes. The man raised an eyebrow at Liam.

'I . . . My name's Connor. I'm new. I was told . . .'

His heart thumped in his chest and he could feel his cheeks flushing. It was natural to be nervous, he knew. This was a big change in his life. But . . . they would help him here. With the things in his head. The things that made him feel that he was different to everyone else. That was why he was here.

He looked around at the dark wood panelling, the big oil paintings on the walls, the wide stairs leading up to a galleried area. Nervous as he was, and grand as this building was, it felt like he was coming home.

'Liam Connor's here,' said the man behind the reception desk. He had picked up a telephone and was talking into it. 'Okay. I'll tell him.' He put the phone down and caught Liam's eye. 'Someone'll be out in a moment,' he said.

Just then an electronic bell rang out and a few seconds later a blue-blazered boy a bit younger than Liam strode out of a nearby corridor. Liam was wearing the same uniform for the first time and it felt odd to him, uncomfortable. This boy looked at home in his. He glanced at Liam and then was gone, just as three more teenagers emerged from another corridor. A door banged open and voices erupted, and soon the reception area was thronged with uniformed pupils, passing from lesson to lesson.

The crowd thinned almost as suddenly as it had formed, and then Liam was left looking at a tall, white-haired man with a sharp face and penetrating pale blue eyes. 'Connor,' said the man. 'Good to see you again. Welcome to the academy. I'm Principal Willoughby.'

Liam remembered him. He had interviewed Liam a few weeks ago. He asked challenging questions and had a prickly manner, but Liam had taken to him straightaway, sensing that he was a good man and NATS a good place. He was going to fit in well here.

Mr Willoughby smiled at him, as if he somehow sensed Liam's positive feelings. 'Come along,' he said. 'Let's get you settled in. I think you're going to like it here.'

★

It all seemed vaguely familiar as he took the tour of the academy.

After a short talk from Willoughby in his office about the importance of teamwork and pushing oneself to the limit, a speech he must have given a thousand times, the principal had introduced Liam to Wallace, one of the Sherborne House prefects. 'Wallace will show you around,' Willoughby had told him.

They toured the corridors of the main building, ambling past classrooms and offices. Wallace was a spotty kid, about the same age as Liam, happy to be missing the last lesson of the afternoon to show the new boy around. 'You've seen it all before I 'spect,' said Wallace, and that was when Liam remembered that he had. Until that point, it had just been a vague sense of *déjà vu* but now Liam recalled seeing all this before on interview day. Dad had driven him down from Norwich and after talking to Mr Willoughby they had been given a similar tour of the academy. No wonder it seemed so familiar.

'Yes, I've seen it once,' said Liam. 'But *you* know. It's all new. It didn't really register at the time.' Lots of his memories were like that: vague, pictures just out of focus, like a sketch yet to be completed or a watercolour painting partly washed away. He supposed it must be like that for everyone.

Just as the bell went for end of lessons, they picked up Liam's case from Reception and headed out along a corridor by the refectory. This was a part of the building that had a different feel to the rest, partly because it was newer and partly because it now thronged with pupils. 'We're in the halls now,' said Wallace. 'The pupils' and house tutors' rooms. All this is a new block, built about twenty years ago. Sherborne House is up this way.'

They went up some stairs. The walls here were painted pale green and there were none of the heavy wood panelling and leaded windows of the main building. They came to the top and Liam put his case down, taking up the handle so he could pull it on its little wheels. He turned right and a split second later Wallace did the same. 'Along here,' his guide said, looking at him curiously. 'Your room's at the end. You're sharing with Linley. A bit of a wazzock, but he's okay really.'

The room wasn't huge, but there was space for two beds, desks and wardrobes. A window to the right looked out over the playing fields towards a strip of dark trees growing out of a drift of gorse.

The boy called Linley lay on the bed under the window, stretched out with his head on his hands, so that his feet almost reached the end of the bed. As well as being tall, Linley was thin, with a dark flop of hair and a steady gaze, now fixed on Liam.

'Well, hello,' he said. He had the kind of accent that suggested a lifetime in public schools, but Liam sensed immediately that it was an affectation. 'I'm Anders Linley. Welcome to NATS, but then I expect you've had all that already, haven't you? Just been on the grand tour? Okay, Wallace, old boy, job done, you can toddle off now.'

As the door closed, Anders turned back to Liam. 'Grunts,' he said dismissively. 'All they're good for, eh?'

Liam knew what he meant. Wallace had been . . . *flat*.

127

Anders, on the other hand, had that something extra, that spark. He could sense that there were shapes in this boy's head.

'Cool,' said Anders, still stretched out lazily on his bed. 'I think we're going to get along just fine. Now, important things: how's your tea-making?'

Liam laughed and turned towards his half of the room. He dragged his case to the foot of the bed and then sat. The mattress was soft and it sagged markedly in the middle, but it would do.

Just then he noticed a cage on one of the desks, with a wheel and a plastic sleeping compartment.

'Ah, you've seen our room-mate,' said Linley. 'My pet hamster, Skiver. Nocturnal, I'm afraid. Makes a dreadful racket through the night . . . You get used to it.'

A hamster. Liam had kept a hamster once, a fat dark thing with a white band across its belly and up each side. It had been a long time ago. He couldn't even remember the creature's name.

Anders was fifteen. He shaved every morning, he claimed, and he had a girlfriend in Rendlesham House. He drank herbal tea and made sure that Liam knew exactly how to make the perfect cup. His father was some kind of ambassador's aide in the Middle East, and when Anders had passed the entry tests his parents had decided he should be schooled at NATS rather than live out there with them. So, because he had passed the admission tests, Anders was what they called a Talent. If he had only got in because his parents were in the diplomatic service he would have been a Grunt, like all the army, navy and RAF kids.

Far better a Talent than a Grunt. Liam knew what he meant. The ones with a spark. The ones with shapes in their heads.

Anders talked a lot too, which didn't help the headache Liam had been trying to fight off all day.

Liam lay down and closed his eyes. Sometimes he got like this. The pounding in his skull. The sense of people pressing in. It was something to do with the things going on in his head, he knew. Something to do with the spark that made him a Talent and not a Grunt.

He put a hand to his forehead, then ran his fingers up through his short, mousy blond hair. He liked his hair longer. He couldn't remember quite why he had gone for this severe crew cut. There was an irregularity in his skull up there, just above the hairline. A dimple. Sometimes it was as if all the pain was focused just below that slight hollow.

Anders was watching him from across the room. 'It's okay,' he said. 'Time for dinner soon. You'll feel better with some food in you.'

He was right. The food made it all better. It was nothing special, only a rather dried-up risotto, but the feel of that food sitting in his stomach was good and Liam's head started to clear.

They sat in the refectory with Tom and Pat McLeish, who had the room next to theirs. The two were twins, although not identical, a year younger than Liam and

Anders. They had only just been granted the room this term – most Year Nines lived in six-bed dorms at the other end of Sherborne's corridor.

The four of them sat eating and exchanging snippets about themselves. Tom and Pat were from Gosport and had been at NATS for three years now. They were Talents, of course. The Grunts and Talents tended to do everything separately.

Liam told them he had been staying with Aunt Katherine in Norwich, and before that had lived there with his father and gone to Hewitt School.

'What about your mum?' asked Tom. 'Our parents divorced, but they're back together again now.'

'She died years ago,' said Liam. 'I can hardly remember her.' He saw the embarrassed looks on the others' faces and added hurriedly, 'It's no big deal. Or at least, not now. It was a long time ago. I was only about six when it all happened.'

He was used to passing it off lightly like that. It was a long time ago and it was almost true that it was no big deal to him now. He had lived more than half of his life without her.

'So, who's this, then?' A girl seated herself in the space next to Anders. She had a gently rounded face and a mass of straw-blonde hair down to her shoulders. She pushed her tray forward and rested her elbows on the table, studying Liam closely.

Anders leaned towards her and put a hand on her arm. 'This is the new chap,' he said. 'I told you: my new tea-maker.'

She patted his hand. 'And do you know, Anders, dear? I bet if he's like all the rest of us, he's probably got a name, hasn't he?'

'I'm Liam. Liam Connor.'

'Pleased to meet you, Liam,' she said. 'I'm Hayley Warren. You just ignore Anders. It's usually best.'

They worked them hard at NATS. He had been warned about that: it was a high-pressure school. Everyone worked long hours, and if you were there on the Talented and Special programme there were extra demands with all the testing. If you didn't make the grade you were filtered out. Lots of pupils only lasted a term or two before they were rejected, and you always had to be able to demonstrate that you were making progress.

They started lessons at eight in the morning and worked through until four. They ate dinner at five, then from six to nine there were all kinds of organized activities, a lot of which turned out to be some form of training or testing, or yet more cramming of academic subjects. On the first evening, Liam found himself in the computer games suite, and even there he sensed that these games, with their challenges and puzzles, were just another form of assessment. Was each triumph, each gained or lost life, fed through to the school tracking system and marked against your record?

Anders and Hayley were a funny pair. Anders was going to be a good friend, Liam thought. He was always around, always helpful in his strangely offhand way. And Hayley was fun, with her gentle digs at them both. She was a nervous person, Liam came to realize, twitchy like a sparrow. They both had the spark. Sometimes it felt like Liam had been reunited with a couple of old friends, but often Anders and Hayley would leave him on his own and slip away together – at lunchtimes and in the hour's free time between the last lesson and dinner.

On the Thursday of his first week, Liam was called down to the principal's office.

He knocked and was invited to enter.

'Connor,' said Principal Willoughby from behind his wide desk. There were a few papers scattered across the desk's green leather surface, and a flat computer screen standing to one side. 'Come in, come in. How are you finding your first week at the academy?'

'Okay, sir. I mean, it's fine, sir.'

'Good.' Willoughby pointed a finger at his computer screen. 'As you know, we've been testing you this week, as we do with all new arrivals. We have to be sure that the right choices have been made. I've been looking at your results.'

Liam swallowed. So this was it. Not even a week here and he was falling behind. Surely they wouldn't turf him out so soon?

'Relax, Connor. You have a very interesting set of results. We will be paying you close attention during what I expect will be a long stay at the academy. Have you given any thought to extra-curricular activities? There's a lot on offer.'

Liam shrugged, then realized that probably wasn't an impressive response. Was even this interview some kind of test? 'There's such a lot to choose from,' he said.

'You should choose carefully,' Principal Willoughby told him. 'We're considering fast-tracking you into Senior House if you make the progress we anticipate. You should choose activities that would support this move.' The principal paused, then added, 'I'd recommend the Elite Forces Cadets.'

Liam nodded. He knew nothing of the cadets, but he was game to try anything.

'Your room-mate, Linley, is in the Elites,' said Principal Willoughby. 'Ask him about it. He'll tell you how to enrol. There's a meeting on Saturday. You should join.'

'Sir. I'll talk to Linley.'

Now Willoughby smiled. Liam had a sudden feeling that a secret was being kept from him. 'In case you needed persuading,' said the principal, 'I thought you might like to meet one of our new consultants. He's working over at the camp with the Wolsey Point Preservation Trust and he'll be running some of the Elites' sessions for us. We're very lucky to have him.'

The door opened and a man walked in. He was a thin man, with dark blond hair, a square chin and a friendly, open smile.

'Dad!'

Liam turned and had hugged his father before he remembered himself and where he was. Embarrassed, he stepped back, but then he saw that Willoughby was smiling too. Maybe Liam would be seeing a lot more of his father, after all.

13

Out with the Elites

They keep these kids imprisoned as effectively as if they were under lock and key. They must have their reasons, wouldn't you think? Maybe it's a bit like dangerous chemicals and industrial processes: the modern world wouldn't work without them, but they need to be kept away from the rest of us, behind protective barriers. They have to be contained.

Friday evening. Liam wandered on his own after school. He found that there was a network of paths through the gorse and brambles that grew beneath the pine trees and evergreen oaks.

Some went all the way down to the creek. From there, Liam could look across to the bulging spit of land known as Wolsey Point. He could see a few of the old military buildings out there. His father was working on a special project in the old Ministry of Defence site on the Point, something to do with enhancement and containment of dangerous resources, he had told Liam enigmatically. They would see more of it on Saturday, when the Elite Cadet Force was due to visit the Point.

He wandered back up through the trees, past a blackened area where someone had lit a fire, contained by round stones.

After a time, he came to a clearing where a strange old pine tree grew. Three trunks emerged at ground level, although from the way they were joined at the base it was clearly a single tree and not three growing closely together. Unlike the other pines, horizontal branches came out from this one from low down, and now he realized that someone was sitting on one of these boughs.

Hayley.

She spotted him and waved, beckoning him to come over.

'End of the week,' said Liam. 'Seems like a long one.'

'Yeah, wasn't it?' said Hayley.

He remembered that she was a member of the Elites and was about to ask her about it, when she spoke first.

'Tell me,' she said. 'You're new here. You're seeing it all for the first time. Me. I've been here for four years. It's like, all there is, you know?' She sucked on her lower lip, then went on. 'Don't you find this place a bit creepy? Like they're always watching you? Playing with your head?'

Liam shrugged. Of course they did. They were being measured and monitored all the time. That was what they *did* at NATS. It was good, wasn't it?

'I'm new,' he said.

She smiled uneasily.

Just then, Anders marched into the clearing. He gave Liam a hard look. 'Connor,' he said. Then to Hayley he added, 'What's he doing here?'

'I . . . I just wandered by,' said Liam, realizing that his room-mate might think he was some kind of a rival. He liked Hayley but . . . well, he was no rival.

Anders flicked his head towards the path he had just emerged from. 'Well, I'll tell you what, Mr Connor. Why don't you just wander off again? This is our place. Hayley and me. Three's a crowd and all that.'

Liam shrugged and moved away along the path. He liked this place with the three-trunked tree. He felt comfortable here. It seemed to stir deep memories of somewhere similar. It didn't matter, though. He didn't want to get in the way of Anders and Hayley. It was their place, not his. He carried on, scuffing his feet in the sandy soil and listening to the cries of the jackdaws high up in the trees.

They met in the Junior Common Room at nine on the Saturday morning. 'Elite Cadet Corps' seemed a strange name for this odd assortment of pupils. The twins, Tom and Pat, were here, along with Anders and Hayley, a Japanese girl called Tsuki and some others Liam didn't know. Most were Talents, but Liam was pretty sure that at least two of them lacked the spark and must be Grunts. This group contained neither the most athletic nor the brightest pupils, but there must be something that bound them together. Liam wondered if they were all being fast-tracked into Senior House, but that didn't seem likely with the two Grunts here.

Two adults joined them: Miss Carver and a certain square-jawed blond man – Liam's father – who smiled at them all as he followed the teacher through the door.

'Okay, Elites, are we all here?' asked Miss Carver, looking around the room. She was one of the younger teachers at NATS: slim and dark-haired and full of spark. She caught Liam's eye now and he blushed. 'Liam,' she said to him. 'Welcome. I'm glad you could join us.'

Hayley kicked him on the ankle.

'Now,' continued Miss Carver, 'as I'm sure the more observant among you have noticed, we have a guest with us today. Mr Connor is a special adviser to NATS. He's here to put you through your paces and to contribute to your development and assessment. Mr Connor has extensive experience in this field and we're very lucky to be able to make use of his expertise. I'm sure you'll all make him feel welcome.'

As soon as Miss Carver had mentioned the guest's name, Anders and Hayley had turned questioning looks on Liam. He gazed down at his feet.

'Right,' said Liam's father. 'Hello, everyone. I've been involved with a project over at Wolsey Camp and today we're all going to go across to work in the research facilities we have over there. It'll be hard work, but it should be fun too. Now: names. I have a list of names here, but I need to put them to faces. Let's go through them. Tsuki Akimoto?'

'Here,' said Tsuki, waving her hand.

'Harry Baker?'

A ginger-haired boy Liam didn't know raised a hand.

'Lucy Chiang?'

★

Mr Connor and Miss Carver led them through the trees to Senior House. A low mutter of conversation broke out as they realized they were actually going inside – Senior House was normally out of bounds.

The interior looked pretty ordinary. There was an open door on the right of the main entrance lobby, and two older pupils sitting on a desk peered out at them.

There was something about this place . . . Suddenly there was more pressure in Liam's head. More shapes.

This place, this building – everything was very intense here.

The entrance lobby was a spacious, wooden-floored area, with lots of doors opening off it and a flight of stairs leading up to the first floor. Miss Carver led them round to the back of the stairs and Liam saw that here another flight led downwards.

They all followed her down.

There was another open area with doors leading off it. This part of the building was all very functional. Where upstairs there had been wooden panelling and leaded windows, here there was a concrete floor and beige plaster on the walls. A thin, grey-haired man sat behind a desk, and he nodded at the two adults as the group gathered at the foot of the stairs.

They passed through a set of sliding doors into a square room, and when they were all inside, Mr Connor pressed a button. The doors closed, and then Liam realized that this room was actually a large lift. With a slight lurch, it started to descend.

He studied those around him curiously. No one seemed

surprised by any of this. There had been a buzz about entering Senior House, but now they all seemed to be taking it in their stride.

'That's right, Liam,' said his father, moving over to join him. 'They've all been here before. It's just starting to come back to them.'

Liam looked at his father now with surprise. How had he known . . .?

His father smiled at him and he relaxed. It was good to be together again.

'The memories are masked,' his father explained. 'The Elites' sessions are very specialized. It's where we really push the candidates for Senior House to see what they're capable of. But we don't want word getting out about these sessions, so the memories are suppressed. The Elites are only allowed to remember them when they come over here on subsequent sessions. It's a very carefully controlled environment.'

'What are we going to do here?'

His father smiled. 'You'll see, Liam. You'll see.'

They were interrupted by the lift coming to a halt. The sliding doors wheezed open, and Liam saw a long corridor ahead of them, illuminated by a strip light that ran along the centre of the ceiling. The floor and walls were concrete.

It was a tunnel. A tunnel that must lead all the way under the creek to Wolsey Point.

There were two open-topped carts here, each with room for one driver and six passengers. They seemed to be made of a grey plastic, with open seating and bars to hold on to. Mr Connor and Miss Carver each took the driving seats and waved the Elites aboard. The vehicles started up with an electric whine and trundled along at a little more than walking pace.

Liam sat, transfixed. His seat faced forward and he hung on to a grab rail in front of him. He stared at the walls as they passed, and at the tunnel ahead. After a time, the floor started to slope gently upwards.

They emerged from the tunnel into a wide indoor parking area, where there were three more of these open electric cars, and about seven or eight Land Rovers and trucks. These were grey too and the doors were marked with the hovering tern logo of the Wolsey Point Preservation Trust.

Liam looked around. They were in some kind of hangar. One end of the building had collapsed and patches of roof were missing. But Liam could see that the damaged areas were strategically propped up with scaffolding. This hangar must look ruined and long-abandoned from the outside, but in reality it was probably as sturdy and safe as it had ever been.

They followed the two corps leaders outside.

A gull flew up, screeching at them in protest, and for a moment Liam felt another of those shocks of *déjà vu*, as if he had been here before. But then the moment passed. The hangar where the tunnel terminated was one of a pair of similar buildings. Here, from the outside, both looked little more than ruins, with roofing collapsed and partly missing, masses of shingle piled up against the seaward walls, windows broken, and wild tangles of gorse and brambles growing all around.

They entered the second hangar.

It was like a small town inside, or a village, at least. Within the shell of the hangar there were three rows of smaller buildings, separated by two concrete streets. The buildings were mostly block-like prefabricated units, although a few were built from brick and concrete, and even had properly tiled roofs. There were cars here too, and people walking between the buildings.

Some of the people were in uniforms. Liam recognized army khaki and RAF blue, but some of the uniforms were ones he didn't know; European, perhaps. Others were in casual clothes, or dark blue overalls. There was even a woman in a grey tracksuit, jogging round the inner perimeter of the hangar.

'Welcome to Wolsey Camp,' said Mr Connor. 'The *real* Wolsey Camp, that is.'

They sat in a classroom, the lights dimmed, Mr Connor standing at the front, surveying them all. The two Grunts had gone off somewhere with Miss Carver.

Out of one window, through the Venetian blinds, Liam could see the inner wall of the hangar and, through a gap in the panelling there, a bank of shingle dotted with white, bell-like flowers with silvery-green leaves. He wondered if there were other hangars like this, here on the Point. He wondered just how big this secret base could be.

A picture flashed up on the white screen behind Mr Connor. A shaved head, seen from above, a small wound marking the skin just above where the hairline would grow back.

'You all have one of these,' said Mr Connor. 'I do too.' He reached up, as if feeling for the scar. 'Go on,' he told them. 'About two knuckles up from where the hair starts.'

Obediently, all ten of the Elites raised hands to their heads, feeling for that strange hollow that Liam knew so well.

'It marks the insertion point of a device developed specially for our kind.'

Our kind. The phrase sounded good to Liam. He wasn't alone. There were others with the shapes in their heads, the spark.

'. . . a device which allows us to take control of the powers we have, as members of the Lost Families. It's vital that we all learn how to restrain our abilities. How to conceal our true nature. It's a question of survival. But at the same time, it's vital that we learn how to use those abilities, and that's the reason we're here today. In a few minutes we'll go through to the psiLab. Each of you will be working with a facilitator who will guide you in the techniques.

'The device normally operates to dampen down your gifts, just like the medication you take in your food over in NATS. The implant is like a little medicine factory, manufacturing the right medications from the ingredients it finds in your blood. Here in the psiLab we will unlock the implant so that it manufactures hormones of a slightly different nature. When this happens you will find that your gifts are given free reign. Don't be frightened by this. Enjoy it. And learn.'

The psiLab was an octagonal room with ten workstations. There were computer screens and keyboards at each unit, along with stacks of what looked like playing cards, and chunky marker pens for writing on the white surfaces of the desks and the walls. There were bottles of water, baskets of fruit and sweets, tissues and cushions and squeezy toys.

Liam's father waved him over to join him while the others seated themselves. Liam noticed that Anders and the two Grunts hadn't gone to workstations either. These three stood to one side with Miss Carver. Anders and the teacher surveyed the room while the Grunts stared blankly ahead.

There were two seats at each workstation, and now a team of what Liam's father had called 'facilitators' filed in. They were wearing the dark blue overalls Liam had noticed before and carrying little hand-held computer devices. They sat, one to each occupied workstation, and started to talk to their allocated Elite cadets.

'Some of these kids have had several sessions here already,' said Liam's father. 'Most have been here at least twice. We'll get you started in a little while.'

'What's that?' asked Liam, pointing towards Tom McLeish's workstation. His facilitator had reached over and placed a hand on the top of his head, staring into the boy's eyes. 'What's he doing to Tom?'

'Unlocking his implant,' said his father. 'Unleashing his gifts. Can't you feel it?'

Liam's father was studying him closely. Around the room, others were having their implants unlocked and Liam felt a sudden lurching sensation in his head as all those sparks ignited, one after another after another . . .

He put a hand to his head, covering his own implant scar. The shapes were moving around, pushing and probing!

He felt a hand on his arm, calming.

'It's okay,' his father told him. 'It all depends on how sensitive you are. You'll be okay in a minute.'

They stood and Liam felt the dizziness starting to recede. He looked at his father. 'What *is* this?' he demanded.

'School,' said his father, chuckling softly. 'This is where our kind are trained and tested: the final exam, if you like. Come with me. I'll show you what I mean.'

They stopped by Tom's workstation. Liam's father nodded at the facilitator, a young man with spectacles and short blond hair. The facilitator held out his palmtop computer and Liam's father took it. He read its display for a time, then handed it back.

There was a stack of cards on the desk between Tom and his facilitator.

'Precog,' said Liam's father. 'Watch.'

The big computer screen was positioned so that they could all see it. It showed four cards, one with a solid circle on its face, one with a hollow square, one with a wavy line and one with an exclamation mark.

'Variation on a standard test,' said Liam's father quietly. 'There was a lot of research on this during the cold war. The Soviet KGB and the American CIA recruited whole legions of the Lost, hoping they could use their precognitive sensing to anticipate what the enemy might do next. Look.'

Tom reached out and touched the computer screen. It must have been touch sensitive, because the card he touched, the exclamation mark, grew to fill the screen. As he did this, the facilitator reached for the top card on the stack. A split second after Tom had made his selection, the facilitator flipped over the top card on to the table.

Exclamation mark.

Tom touched the solid circle next and the facilitator turned the next card to reveal a circle. In the bottom right of the screen, a tally was being kept: '1/1' flipped to '2/2'.

Tom pointed at the circle again, the card was turned . . . '3/3'.

'There are a hundred cards in that set,' said Liam's father, guiding his son away from the workstation with a hand on his shoulder. 'Tom will get something like ninety-five per cent right. Someone without the gift would get about twenty-five per cent.'

They stopped by Tsuki's workstation next. Her facilitator was sitting next to her, and across the desk from them was one of the Grunts. His face was slack and there was a blankness in his eyes, as he sat slumped forward, his hand holding a pen over a sheet of paper. His empty expression was in complete contrast to the absolute concentration on Tsuki's face.

'Tsuki's quite something,' said Liam's father. 'She's travelled halfway round the world to study here.'

Slowly, the Grunt started to make marks on the paper. At first they appeared to be random slashes and strokes, then Liam realized that he was writing in Japanese script. Somehow Tsuki was making his hand move, making him write in a language that was alien to him.

Again, they moved on.

Hayley sat, wide-eyed, staring at a glass tank in front of her. She looked scared. She looked to be on the verge of tears. Her facilitator, a young woman who could not have been more than a handful of years older, was leaning towards her, talking in gentle, coaxing tones.

'Young Ms Warren's an odd one,' said Liam's father, taking the palmtop from the desk to study her notes. 'She's been here more times than anyone else, but never quite makes the breakthrough. She has a unique talent. When she gets it right she can project her own worst fears and give them substance in the real world.'

Just then, Hayley glanced up at Liam and gave an uncertain smile. She didn't want to do this. It didn't require any special powers to see that.

Liam smiled back at her, just as his father went down on his haunches and spoke to Hayley. 'Miss Carver has told me a lot about your abilities,' he said. 'I'd really like to see what you're capable of. Do you think you can do it for me, Hayley? Just once? Just for a second or two?'

He gestured at the tank and Hayley looked where he pointed. She blinked and swallowed loudly.

Liam looked into the tank, wondering what she was trying to do.

Nothing.

Then she gave a little gasp, and, suddenly, in the far corner of the tank there was a spider. It was the size of Liam's hand, and its body and legs were covered in tufts of chestnut bristles. It scrambled at the glass, trying to climb the side of the tank, trying to get out.

Hayley was holding herself tight, tears running down her cheeks, her eyes fixed on the giant spider.

Seconds later, it vanished. All that remained were a few

dusty smears where it had come up against the glass.

Hayley sagged, and her facilitator put an arm round her and rocked her, as if she was comforting a small child.

Liam nodded towards Anders. 'What about him?' he asked. 'What about Anders? Why isn't he taking part?'

'Oh, he's not here to take part,' said Liam's father. 'He's monitoring it all. Anders is part of Willoughby's security operation.'

Liam stared at his room-mate.

His father nodded. 'He's watching you, Hayley, Tsuki and the others. He's watching me too. None of us can be allowed to step out of line. Or at least, we mustn't be caught.'

'Why? What's this all about?'

'Our kind are very useful,' his father told him. 'Like I said, in the cold war we were used by the CIA and the KGB for spying and even out in the war zones around the world. Nothing ever changes. We've been exploited like that throughout history. This operation? Those of you who make the grade will be taken into the service of the government, or of the big corporations. Those who don't will be sent back into normal life, none the wiser. And those who prove to be too dangerous will be eliminated. That's how it is, and how it has always been. We're slaves, Liam. There's no such thing as free choice.

'The elders of the Lost Families have bought security and protection for our kind, but at the price that we are trapped in this cycle of enslavement. Willoughby is a bit of a rogue: the Families allow him to run his own little experiments at NATS as long as he doesn't rock the boat too much. They won't let him upset our masters . . .'

Liam glanced at Anders.

'It's all right,' his father told him. 'Sometimes we can fool them for a little of the time. He doesn't know we're talking. I've blocked him for a short while. You won't remember this, of course. Like the others, your memories of today will be masked at the end of the session. But deep down, Liam, you might hang on to part of it. Do you understand?'

Liam stared at him. In the back of his head he could hear children singing. *London's burning, London's burning. Fire! Fire!* Betrayal, deception. Some deep, distant memory coming back – only to slip out of his grasp before he could pin it down.

He nodded. 'I understand,' he said. 'I think.'

'Good.'

'What about me?' Liam asked. 'Why am I here?'

'You? You're special, Liam. Didn't you know that? You may turn out to be very special indeed. Like Hayley, you have an unusual talent. A rarity. You are what's known as a channeller. You have a lot of the typical talents, but only to a small degree: you can sense other people's minds, but we don't think you can actually read other people very well. You have a little precog. With training you probably have a little telekinetic ability: the power to move objects without touching them. You won't have noticed any of these to any great extent, because the drugs have been suppressing your abilities most of the time.

'Channelling is where we think your real talent lies. It's a sensitivity to other people's talents. We'll try it today: put you to work with Tom, there, and he'll probably hit a ninety-nine or even a hundred per cent success rate. Put you with Tsuki and we'll have that Grunt yapping like a dog and jumping through hoops for the two of you. Here . . .'

He gestured for Hayley's facilitator to stand so that Liam could sit in her chair.

He sat, and Hayley looked at him nervously. She smiled. 'I'd forgotten about all this,' she said to him. 'They make you forget.'

He tried to give her a reassuring smile, but he felt that he was betraying her as he did so.

His father was squatting at their side again. 'Just one more time, Hayley,' he said. 'That was really great, but I want to see it one more time. Liam here is going to help you. He'll make it easy for you. Liam: look at me.'

Liam turned and his father placed a hand on his head. He stared into his father's eyes and felt a rushing sensation, a sliding, a sickness in the pit of his stomach.

Something was different in his head. A blanket had been lifted.

The shapes!

They were crowding him, shouting for his attention. All these people . . . their minds pressing in on him.

Hayley was there. Scared. He was to help her.

'Go on, Hayley. Now,' said Mr Connor, 'do it again.'

There was fear in her thought-shapes. Dread. She was trying to project it, to aim it at the glass tank, to force it all into that confined space.

Liam turned to look. He pushed her fears away into the tank. He was helping her.

In the far corner there was a creature, bigger than last time. Grey. Fur. Twitching nose. Glinting eyes and a long, bare tail. A rat.

It clawed at the glass floor of the tank just as another rat materialized, clambering over its back.

And another. Another.

Liam felt the power rushing through his mind, a wave of exhilaration . . . of possibilities . . .

Rats appeared out of nowhere, piling one on top of another, filling the tank.

Soon there was no more space in the tank, and still Hayley's fear was rushing outwards, channelled into that space.

The side of the tank cracked in one place, then another, and a panel of glass splintered and fell outwards. Rats tumbled out, scrambling in the shards of broken glass, scampering across the desk, dropping to the floor —

Liam felt himself being hauled away, out of the chair, a hand on his head, a smothering shroud clamping round the shapes in his mind. He slumped and was caught in someone's arms.

He looked across to the workstation and saw the shattered glass tank, and Hayley crying in the arms of her facilitator. The rats had vanished, back to wherever they had come from. Liam closed his eyes, dizzy, sick, stunned.

14

Reminders

Dig a deep hole, or go to a quarry and look at the exposed rock face, and you will see that the ground beneath our feet isn't just mud and stone. It's more complex than that. There are layers – what geologists call 'strata'. These layers are deposited over time. If you know how to read them you can read the intimate history of the land.

It's all there, beneath our feet. Hidden by time. You just need to know how to look.

Skiver ran in his plastic wheel. Round and round and round. The wheel rumbled and squeaked and the hamster kept going. He didn't know any better.

Liam lay awake, staring at the night sky through the window.

'So, what did you make of the Elite Cadet Corps?' asked Anders, lying awake too, his hands behind his head.

'It was okay,' said Liam. 'Filled a Saturday, I suppose.'

Anders laughed. 'Do you remember much about it?' he asked. 'It always seems to go by in such a whirl.'

Liam thought back to the day they had spent out on the Point. In all honesty, he couldn't remember very much at all. As Anders said, the day seemed to have passed in a whirl. He remembered running on an orienteering course through the shingle banks, and eating lunch out by the sea. He was sure they'd done more than that, but the specifics eluded him. For some reason, that disturbed him.

'Not much,' said Liam. 'Too tired.' Somewhere, deep in his mind, he felt shapes moving, probing, and then they were gone.

In the morning, after breakfast with Anders and Hayley, he wandered back to the room alone. Hayley seemed twitchier than usual today, distracted somehow. She wouldn't say what was the matter, though. Liam had only known her for a week – she might often be like this, for all he knew.

Back in his room, he flicked through a maths book, then reached into his top desk drawer for his mobile phone. He flipped it open and saw that he had a message from a number he didn't recognize.

He opened it and stared at the text.

'Things are not what they seem.'

What could that mean? The phrase seemed familiar, but Liam couldn't quite place where he had heard or read it before.

He thought about his new life here at NATS. Everything seemed to be going well. He had no reason to suspect that anything odd was going on. So what did the message mean?

He selected the options for the message and chose to call the number it had been sent from.

There was silence for a few seconds, then a woman's voice said, 'You have dialled an incorrect number. Please check the number and redial. You have dialled an in–' He cancelled the call, cutting the recorded message off in mid-sentence as it started to repeat itself.

Things are not what they seem.

Just then there was a knock and the door pushed open. It was Wallace.

'A corridor prefect's job is never done, eh?' said Liam.

Wallace grinned. 'Willoughby,' he said. 'He wants to see you.'

Liam headed down through the modern extension and into the older part of the house. He wondered what this could be about. Principal Willoughby seemed to be paying very close attention to his early days in the academy. He wondered if the principal did this for every new pupil.

He knocked on the dark wooden door.

'Enter.'

Willoughby was there behind his wide desk. 'Come in, come in,' he said, as Liam opened the door. 'I have some good news for you, Connor.'

Liam stopped in front of his desk and waited for the principal to continue.

'You came to the academy late,' said Willoughby. 'Normally we like to enter new students on the Talented and Special programme well before Year Ten. But that's by the by. We're going to move you up to Senior House, Connor. I know you've only just started to settle in, but after lunch I want you to pack your bags and take them over to Senior House. You know where it is, don't you?

Miss Carver is the house tutor on duty today. Ask for her and she'll sort you out. Okay? Good. That's all.'

Willoughby turned back to his computer screen and tapped something on his keyboard to kill the screen saver.

Liam turned and left the office.

They had really meant it when they talked about fast-tracking him. He wondered what it meant. What was so special about him? Why were they treating him this way?

He walked.

He was still new here and, while everyone had been friendly, he couldn't really claim that he had made any proper friends yet. Coming here halfway through term, he was stepping into established routines. People had the things they did, the friends they did them with. He hadn't quite found a way to fit in.

So he walked.

He could have gone back to his room, he supposed. Pack his suitcase ready for this afternoon's move. But he had only been here a week and he'd barely had time to *un*pack. It wouldn't take him long to throw everything into the case again for the short walk through the trees to Senior House.

He skirted round the playing fields. There was a cricket match going on. The scoreboard read 84 for 5, but he didn't know who was playing. He had always done well in team games. Never the star player, but still he had been a popular pick. When Liam was in a team everyone around him seemed to play much better. He seemed to have a knack for getting the best out of people.

He cut through the gorse on one of the many trails without really thinking. It was only when he recognized the three trunks of a lone tree ahead that he realized he had headed for the old pine Anders called Three Trunker. It just seemed natural to come here, even though it was Anders' and Hayley's place, not his.

He considered turning back, but decided against it.

If they were here they might be okay about him wandering by. He could tell them about Senior House. Anders would probably be pleased that the double room would be his own again. Or his and his hamster's, at any rate.

And if they weren't here . . . well, there was something special about this place. Something that reached deep inside Liam: a sense of peace, of belonging, a sense of *memory*.

Still he hesitated as he came to the edge of the clearing where Three Trunker grew. He looked carefully and felt a surge of relief when he was sure that he was alone. He remembered how twitchy Hayley had been this morning at breakfast. Maybe she and Anders had argued.

He sat on the low, horizontal bough with his back to one of the three trunks. It was funny how boarding school could be such a lonely place, when you were almost always surrounded by people.

This memory thing was bothering him, he realized. He seemed to have spent the last week stuck completely in the present time . . . Everything was short-term: he could remember lessons on Friday, he could remember the surprise when his father had walked through Principal Willoughby's door on Thursday, he could remember climbing out of the taxi on Monday after the journey down from Norwich.

But before that?

Suddenly everything became fuzzy, vague. He had stayed with Aunt Katherine for a few weeks, but that was exactly how he remembered it: he remembered *having stayed* with Kath. He couldn't remember the detail. He couldn't remember any incidents, any things they had done, any place they had gone, even anything they had watched on TV or any music they had listened to. It was almost as if someone had told him about it, rather than that he had actually experienced it.

And now . . . This was what disturbed him, he realized. Now most of yesterday was a similar blur: sketchy outlines of going with the Elites to Wolsey Point, but no detail, no substance.

Was he ill? Was he suffering some kind of mental decay that had eaten away at his more distant memories and was now taking chunks out of even recent events?

He remembered Hayley's questions when he'd found her here a couple of days ago. She had asked if he felt as if he was being watched, if he felt as if his head was being messed with. Maybe his feelings were normal, then. Maybe everyone felt like this about how hard it was to hold on to memories. It was stupid of him to worry about it.

He tipped his head up. The sun had broken through now, and it was hot on his skin. Everything seemed better when the sun shone like this.

Teething problems. That was all it was. Settling in. It

was only natural that he should feel disoriented, confused.

A little time later, a gull swooped in low and landed on the sandy ground a short distance away. It was a smart bird, with sooty grey wings, yellow legs and beak, and a pure, crisp white body. It stared at him with beady yellow eyes, then threw its head back and gave a long-drawn-out screeching cry.

Liam felt a dizzy lurch.

Ruined building . . . broken roof . . . sand piled up on a concrete floor . . . a gull peering in through the gap in the roof, then throwing its head back to cry out to the world.

And he remembered this place too: the three-trunked pine. A sudden flash, a crystal clear memory: sitting down there on the ground with Hayley, with Anders up here in the tree, watching them both. Hanging out here with the two of them. Their place. All three of them.

Other fragments came to him, then. A row of white cottages, lined up at a jaunty angle across a shingle beach. A man with balding silver hair and thick-framed glasses in one of those cottages. Fire. Something to do with fire. 'London's burning.' Children's voices, singing that song as his father betrayed him . . .

Liam felt dizzy.

All those fragments locked up in his head. He had saved them. He had saved these memories when someone had been doing things to his mind. He had clung on to them desperately.

Why?

There was something awful, a deep, deep dreadful fear, wrapped up with those memories, or with the act of clinging on to those memories – the *memory* of those memories. Some terrible threat.

He looked around the clearing, but he was still alone.

They can get into your head and do things . . . But who?

And why? Why did he have memories of some past life buried away deep in the layers of his mind?

'You okay?' Anders strolled into the room, and Liam flinched like a startled rabbit.

'Yes,' he said. 'I'm okay.'

'You seem jumpy, that's all.'

Liam shrugged. There were shapes in his head again and he tried to visualize himself pushing them away. 'I suppose I am,' he said. 'I saw old Willoughby this morning. Looks like you'll be getting this room back to yourself again.'

For a moment, Anders was thrown. 'You mean . . .?'

Liam gave a short laugh. 'That's right,' he said. 'They're kicking me out.' Then he added, 'All the way to Senior House.'

Anders laughed too. 'Blimey,' he said. 'You don't hang around, do you? You make the rest of us look like Grunts.'

Suddenly, he became serious. He came over and held his hand out for Liam to shake. 'Well, old man. Looks like you've made the grade. Good for you. Wait till the others all hear at lunch!' With that, Anders wandered off again. Spreading the word, Liam presumed.

He finished packing, gathering his school things off the desk and slipping them into the elasticated, external pocket of his big case.

He took his phone from the desk drawer and flipped it open, remembering that odd message. *Things are not what they seem.* Perhaps it had been some kind of warning about Senior House?

A reminder had popped up on the screen. He opened it: '13 June. Mum's birthday.' Today was the eleventh: it was his mother's birthday in two days' time.

He sat at the foot of his bed.

Mum had died nine years ago.

He didn't know her. He hardly remembered her. She was just a hole in his life, a space where other people had someone but he didn't.

So why would he have entered her birthday on his phone's calendar? Why would he have set it to remind him like this?

He tried to picture her. Tried to remember the things they must have done together. It was so long ago and he had only been young.

It was all so vague.

There was a phone number included in the reminder.

His thumb hovered over the keypad, but he didn't dial it.

He wasn't ready for this.

He couldn't key the number.

He just couldn't.

15

Another New Beginning

Senior House was a community on its own, isolated within the larger community of the National Academy for the Talented and Special. Those who were talented enough, and who passed all the tests they were set, were marked out as special, and Senior House was where they were destined to end up.

Fail the main school and you would be sent back out into the so-called normal world.

Fail Senior House and . . . you had to be dealt with in other ways.

Miss Carver was waiting for him outside Senior House. 'Liam,' she said as he trudged through the trees, dragging his suitcase along the sandy trail. 'Welcome!'

She turned and he followed her up the steps and into the house.

Immediately he was struck by the intensity of this building, the sense of other minds occupying this space. He felt the strong need to guard himself, to protect his own mind from the intrusive presence of these others.

'It's okay,' said Miss Carver. 'Most of us are hit by the

160

atmosphere of Senior House. So many of our kind all together under one roof. You'll get used to it.'

Liam stared at her, struck by the openness of her words. *Our kind.*

'Halls are up here,' she said, heading up the stairs. He followed her to the first floor and along a corridor. 'There are only eleven students in Senior House right now,' she told him. 'We're very selective. There's always at least one house tutor on duty, usually me or Mr Pullinger.'

She pointed at a door as they passed. 'Bathrooms,' she said. 'Mixed, so remember to lock the door.' She pushed the next door open and waved a hand. 'Kitchen,' she said. 'For tea and coffee and the like.' There was a girl in there watching over a boiling kettle. She looked up and smiled.

'Your room's along here.'

They came to the end of the corridor and Miss Carver knocked on one of the two doors there. There was no reply. She took a key from her pocket and opened the door. 'That boy,' she said, shaking her head. 'You're sharing with Luc. I told him we were coming, but it looks like he's off wandering again . . . You'll get used to him.'

The room was a little larger than the one he had shared with Anders in Sherborne House. The furniture was the same, although the layout was a little different, with the two desks side by side along the far wall. The other boy's belongings were spread about across one desk and one of the beds. There were pot plants too. A spider plant was up on top of one of the wardrobes, baby plantlets tumbling down towards the light from the window. Other plants grew in pots on his room-mate's desk and from a plant stand by the window.

'You'll be okay?' said Miss Carver from the doorway. 'Dinner downstairs at five. I'll leave you to settle in.'

Alone, Liam hauled his case across to the foot of the unused bed.

He went to look out of the half-open sash window.

And there, climbing up an iron drainpipe towards the window, was a tall, blond boy, maybe a year or so older than Liam. Liam recognized him instantly, as just about the only Senior they ever saw in the main part of the school, usually wandering around as if he was lost.

The boy looked up and paused, grinning.

'Hello,' he said. 'I am Luc Renaudier and I am to be your new room buddy.'

Liam sat back on his new bed as Luc tumbled in through the window, all arms and legs, and then stood, brushing himself down.

'Please, excuse my strange entry,' he said. Luc spoke with a thick French accent. 'I like to climb. I like to practise. I can climb a flagpole. Do you believe that? I have climbed both flagpoles on the academy towers. You believe me? You can verify my claim. You climb those poles, you will find my initials carved with a penknife, right there at the top of the poles. Both of them. I am good, you see. But . . .' He shrugged. 'I practise. You practise, you get better, yes?'

'Yes,' said Liam. 'Yes, of course.'

Luc nodded towards the suitcase. 'Yours, yes? You have

all that you need? You must ask if there is anything, yes? You want to talk? Okay, outside. I see you there?'

He sprung up on to the window ledge, then pivoted out on his hands. It looked as if he had just jumped clear, but when Liam went across he saw that his new room-mate was shinning down the drainpipe again.

Liam took the corridor and stairs, locking his room's door with the key Miss Carver had given him.

He found Luc sitting on the trunk of a fallen pine, deep in the shade of the trees. He had a fir cone and was prising the scales off one by one. He peered at Liam as he approached. He seemed more wary now, out in the open.

'You must forgive me,' he said as Liam sat further along the fallen tree. 'I show off. It is a bad way of pretending I am not nervous.'

Liam waited for him to continue.

'What kind of freak are you going to be, eh?' Luc laughed. 'The people in this place . . .' He leaned towards Liam and continued in a stage whisper, 'There are some *strange* people here, no? I get around a lot. I see them. I do not know what kind of strange person they will be putting in my room with me, so I am nervous and I do some showing off. You will forgive me?'

Liam shrugged. 'You don't know how strange I am yet,' he joked.

'And you me, no?' Luc laughed. 'So. You tell me yours and I will tell you mine, yes?'

Liam must have looked blank, because Luc continued, 'Our aptitudes. The gifts we have in our heads, yes?'

Liam shrugged again.

'I go first, then,' said Luc. 'My most special gift is that I get past people. I *deflect*. I would make a very good *cambrioleur* – robber of houses. I can get in and out of places and if anyone is there I can send their attention the other way. They seek him here, they seek him there, that most elusive Luc Renaudier! Yes?'

Liam remembered Miss Carver's reaction when she had shown him to the room he was to share with Luc. *That boy.* 'Must come in useful,' said Liam.

Luc nodded seriously. 'It is a thing in my family,' he said. 'I come from a small village near Guérande. We harvest salt, you know. But also, my people, we do not like to be pushed around. When the Nazis came to my country in the Second World War my grandparents fought against them. They were in the Maquis, the Resistance, and the family gift was very important to them. It kept them alive. But they did not have the opportunities of self-improvement that we have here. The gift was as it was, a talent that was . . . unripe. Here, we ripen, no?'

'I've seen you about the place,' said Liam. 'Last week. You're the only Senior I've seen in the main school.'

'They like to keep we Seniors apart,' said Luc. 'But I do not like to be fenced in, so I slip away from time to time. I told you: we do not like to be pushed around, we Renaudiers. So: you. What is yours? Why is it that you are here in Senior House? What is the gift in your head?'

Liam thought. Somewhere deep down he knew, but like so many of his memories that knowledge was deep, obscured. He couldn't quite reach it. 'I don't know,' he said finally. He remembered Willoughby telling him he had been selected for Senior House this morning. 'I don't know what it is, but I think it might be something very special.'

That evening, they ate in a dining room on the ground floor of Senior House. Liam sat at a table with Luc and a younger boy called Morton.

They swapped stories of their past. Both Luc and Morton had been at NATS for about three years, each progressing from the main school to Senior House after only a term.

'One week?' said Morton, after Liam told them how recently he had arrived at NATS. 'That's a record, isn't it? Hey, Luc, we're in the presence of greatness.'

'A week?' said Luc, eyeing Liam curiously. 'I think . . . I think that it must have been someone else like you I saw before, then . . .'

As they talked, the memory thing bothered Liam again.

Luc told them of his home in the heart of the Marais Salants, a landscape of lagoons where families like his own hoed the clay up into ridges to make channels and shallow pools where the seawater would evaporate in the sun, giving up its salt to be harvested. He told them of the avocets and stilts, spindly legged wading birds which specialized in feeding in these pools, and of the terns that would swoop and dive at your head when you were out working the brine.

Morton talked of growing up in the heart of a northern city, the posh kid who was always picked on. Trying to avoid getting beaten up by the Asian gangs, or the skinheads, or by his older brother's smack-head friends. His brother hadn't been able to cope with his own talent, but Morton had used his to defend himself: he discovered he could hurt people, fill their brains with pain. He didn't like to do it, but sometimes it had been his only defence.

These memories were intense and vivid for Luc and Morton. They had substance, detail, passion.

Liam had only a few sharp memories from before last week, and these were fragments: Three Trunker, that gull on the Point, some white cottages, children singing . . .

He went to bed early. It had been a long day and he was tired. He wondered when anything would seem normal again.

Lessons in Senior House were organized differently to those in the main school. Classes were small at NATS, usually no more than a dozen pupils at a time, but here in Senior House even that wasn't possible.

First thing Monday morning, Liam spent half an hour establishing his new timetable with Miss Carver. There were all the normal curriculum subjects, and Miss Carver told him he would be sitting the standard exams when he was sixteen, just as if he was at any other school in the country. But there were to be extra lessons too. A lot of these were one-to-one counselling sessions with Miss Carver, Mr Pullinger and others, including a Mr Connor. 'We'll be working on your areas of strength,' said Miss Carver. 'Refining your talents. You'll find that it's hard work here in Senior House, but I think you'll take to it.'

It felt good to have Miss Carver saying these things.

Liam felt a rush of warmth from her with the words. She was going to help him. He could trust her with anything.

Later in the morning, she took him through to a classroom. 'We'll be giving you an induction session now, Liam. Explaining a bit more about how Senior House operates, but also about the wider picture: our talents, the medication regime, the place of the Lost Families of Mankind. You'll find that you know some of this already and that it will all come back to you during the session.'

Liam sat at one of the six desks.

Miss Carver glanced at her watch. 'We'll just give it a few more minutes. We have another new member of Senior House today, so this session will be for the two of you.'

Another one? Liam wondered who it might be. He'd only been in the main school for a week, so he didn't know many people there. He sat and looked out of the window.

A short time later, the door opened and a girl stood there, two suitcases on the floor behind her, blocking the corridor.

'Hi, Liam. Miss Carver. Am I in the right place? They just said . . .'

'You are,' said Miss Carver. 'Come on in. Best move your cases out of the way. I'll settle you in your room later. Come on in, Hayley. Welcome to Senior House.'

16

Green Eyes

Sometimes you just know you can trust someone. You can tell straightaway that a person – Hayley, for instance – is someone you would trust with your life, a person with whom you will be sharing secrets and jokes and embarrassing stories for many years to come.

Most of the time, though, you should beware.

She came into the classroom, dragging her two cases behind her, and sat at the desk next to Liam's with a big grin on her face.

Miss Carver looked at the two of them, then sighed. 'Okay,' she said. 'I'll give you five minutes.'

As Miss Carver left the room, Hayley said, 'Well. Here I am, then. I never thought I'd see this place from the inside, know what I mean?'

Liam laughed. 'You'll get used to it,' he said, sounding like the old hand that he clearly wasn't.

'Aren't you going to ask what I'm doing here?'

'You've been promoted,' said Liam. 'Well done.'

Hayley nodded. 'Old Willoughby told me this morning. It was after the last Elites session. He told me I'd suddenly made a lot of progress and that I'd benefit from the more targeted coaching available in Senior House. That's what he said. My old man'll be so pleased!'

'So,' said Liam, wondering, 'what was so special about Elites on Saturday? Do you remember what it was that you did well?'

She stopped to think. 'Nah,' she said. 'Don't remember much about it at all. It's like that, though. Tires you out. All runs together, doesn't it?'

So, it wasn't only Liam's memories that went muddy and unclear. He wasn't sure if he should feel good about that or not.

'Tell you one thing, though,' said Hayley, leaning towards him across the gap between the desks. 'You should have seen Anders' face! He's mad. Here we are, you and me, hand-picked for Senior House and he's left back there in playgroup. He thinks you're after me. He's jealous as hell.'

Liam blushed. He couldn't help himself.

'You're not, are you?' asked Hayley.

'No!' Liam protested. He couldn't tell from her tone whether she was serious or teasing. Probably both.

'All right, all right. Don't worry about my feelings or anything. You should have seen him, though. I've got a new nickname for him. Green-eyed Monster. He's silly. I told him it's him or no one for me, but he's still jealous. Kind of sweet, really, don't you think?'

Miss Carver walked back in at that moment. 'Okay?' she said. 'Let's get on with this session.' She went up to the front of the class and turned to them, suddenly looking serious. 'I'm going to tell you about yourselves, and about this place,' she said. 'I'm going to tell you some things you already know, and some things that will be a complete surprise. After this session you will understand our purpose, the reason our kind lead the lives we do.'

She told them about the special talents that some people – 'our kind of people' – were born with. The ability to sense the thought patterns of others, so that you could read mood, intention, even some unguarded thoughts. The ability to predict events a split second, or sometimes more, before they happened. The ability to take control of other people's muscles. To reach into people's minds and change what you find. To affect what people see and hear – Liam thought of Luc's claimed ability to distract people. To project images and even objects so that your thoughts take on substance for a time. 'This is what you are best at, Hayley: you can project your own fears so that they take on physical form.'

Liam looked at Hayley, saw the understanding. Somewhere inside, she knew this already – Miss Carver was just unlocking the knowledge.

'And me?' he asked.

'You . . .' said Miss Carver, staring at him intensely – almost *hungrily* – 'you make us strong, Liam. You make us very strong.'

He turned away from her look, confused. What could she mean? He opened his mouth to ask her to explain, but already she had moved on.

She told them about the drugs. Medicines used to suppress these gifts, so that children could grow up without their talents erupting and causing them problems. And medicines that would enhance the gifts, bringing them out and reinforcing them. The medication was usually concealed in food. 'Secrecy is a part of how we must live,' Miss Carver told them.

'There are side effects too,' said Miss Carver. 'Consequences of being as we are. Our kind tend to be vulnerable to disease, particularly the illnesses of ageing. Without these medicines you would have a life expectancy of maybe forty-five years. The medicines should give us a normal lifespan, as long as we take them continuously.'

She told them about the implants, encouraging them to feel their own and each other's scalps, just two knuckles above the hairline. Liam put his hand on Hayley's head, running his forefinger lightly up her scalp, through the thick mat of hair, until he found a dimple, just like the one on his own head.

Sitting there, with his hand on Hayley's head, he had a sudden flash of memory, of seeing someone do something very similar before. A room like this . . . someone else doing this to Hayley. And then the memory was gone.

He sat back in his seat as Miss Carver explained that when they were fully functional the implants would be used to manufacture the right medicines from raw ingredients found in their own bloodstreams.

Miss Carver's eyes lit up at that point. 'It is one step towards liberating our kind,' she said. 'Those of us trained in the use of our implants aren't tied into the supply of medications any more.'

She told them about the Lost Families of Mankind.

'What about womankind?' muttered Hayley, but their tutor continued.

'The talented are different,' she said. 'We are a different race. A different *species*, depending on your definitions. Our people have been lost among the flotsam of mankind for generations, but now programmes like this are identifying the talented, the Lost, and bringing us together again. Our kind is regrouping, working in the greater service of mankind as a whole. And that is the purpose of NATS. That is why we are here. Finding and nurturing our own and putting them into the service of the greater good.'

Why did she talk of liberation when her words made Liam think of slavery? There was no free choice in this. They were being used, enslaved. Again, he felt that he had heard that argument somewhere before, but he wasn't sure where.

Miss Carver was smiling at them.

'There,' she said. 'I think that's enough for now. I expect you'll have lots of questions, either now or later. We'll take a break, then you can quiz me all you like afterwards. During the rest of this week you'll have plenty of chances to revisit this with me and your other tutors. Okay?'

In the hour before dinner, Liam started to unlock his memories.

Alone.

He felt the need to be by himself after a day in Senior House with all those presences intruding on his thoughts. It could swamp you quite easily. Let them in and you would be lost in the chaos of other people's thought-shapes.

He wondered if they had changed the medication since he had moved up to Senior. Relaxed it, or changed the balance somehow to lift some of the blocks on his gifts. Maybe his implant had been activated in some limited way.

Whatever . . . he had to escape that atmosphere, for a time, at least.

He walked by the creek.

He thought about the reminder on his phone. Mum's birthday. Why would he have such a reminder, so many years after her death? He had checked through the phone, but other than this one reminder it had been quite conspicuously blank: no stored numbers or old texts, no other reminders. It was like a new phone, or one that had been cleared. So why *this* reminder? It was as if someone was leading him on. Perhaps the same person who had sent that mysterious message. Someone trying to help him unlock his own mind . . .

Yet again, he went over the memories he had managed to recover. From *before*. The gull screaming on a broken roof – somewhere on Wolsey Point, he thought. Hanging out at Three Trunker with Anders and Hayley when it had been *their* special place, not just Anders' and Hayley's. The white cottages on the beach. Children singing 'London's Burning' while hands closed on Liam's arms, trapping him, and all the time his father watched, not raising a finger to help him.

These memories had a substance to them that none of his other memories from before NATS had.

There had been a key, he realized. Those memories had flashed back when that gull landed near to him and called, triggering a burst of recollection.

Today, in the induction session with Miss Carver . . .

He remembered sliding his forefinger up through Hayley's blonde hair to find the mark where her implant had been inserted. At that moment, another memory had flashed up at him from the depths of his mind. Something very similar: not with his own hand on Hayley's head, but someone else doing so while he watched.

A room, with computer screens and bowls of fruit and sweets. White, wipe-clean desktops you could write on with marker pens.

That was how they switched on the implants: something with the hands on the heads so that you could project images of rats – no, *real* rats – into a glass tank on the desk and wait for it to burst . . .

He remembered Hayley's terrified face. The tears.

He remembered Tsuki's steely concentration as she made a zombie-like Grunt write in Japanese script.

He remembered Miss Carver and Anders watching all this from the side of the room.

Security – watching you . . . watching us . . .

Anders had spied on them in the school, Liam realized. No doubt using all the skills and techniques they developed here. He wondered what his former room-mate must have read from his mind. What secret thoughts had he given away?

Whatever it was, he had only been at NATS for a week and he supposed he must have passed. Or, at least, not given away anything incriminating.

Not that he had any incriminating secrets in his head. Not that he knew of.

★

Liam was quiet at dinner, and even Hayley couldn't provoke more than the occasional grunted response from him.

Luc tried to jolly him along too, but then he would, wouldn't he?

If they roomed him with a mind-reading spy to start with, why not continue here in Senior House?

Liam refused to be drawn. He ate and watched as Hayley made friends with Luc, Morton and a girl called Briony. He left early, making the excuse that he was tired.

Up in the room he shared with Luc, he lay down on his bed and stared at the ceiling. He wouldn't sleep, he knew. It was light now – nearly the longest day – and even later, when it became dark, he knew sleep wouldn't come.

He should just go to his father and ask to leave. Go back to Norwich and a normal school.

That would never happen, though. His father was working down here now and Liam could hardly live permanently on Aunt Kath's sofa.

Anyway, he knew he was in deep here. They were not going to allow him just to walk away.

The door opened and Luc was there. The French boy hesitated in the doorway, then came in. 'You are unwell?' he said.

Liam said nothing.

Luc sat on the window ledge. 'Why is it that you are angry?' He seemed hesitant, puzzled. He had obviously been trained by the same people that had trained Liam's last spying room-mate. He was very convincing.

'I don't want to talk about it,' said Liam, turning his face away from Luc's searching gaze.

'Okay,' said Luc. 'I would go to my room and leave you, but . . .'

'You people are very good,' said Liam. He couldn't contain it any longer. 'Very convincing.'

'I am sorry?'

'My last room-mate was a spy too.'

'I . . .'

Liam turned now and saw that Luc was staring at him. He was trying not to laugh.

'You think . . .?'

The effort was too great and the boy burst out laughing. 'I am sorry,' he said. 'You think . . .' He put a hand up, miming apologies. 'You are right to be suspicious, my friend,' said Luc finally. 'Be watchful and suspect everyone, yes? It is the only way. But really . . . Forgive me, but you are not the most observant of us all, are you? No, look at me: I am one of the good guys! But I would say that, wouldn't I?' He laughed again.

'No,' he continued, still chuckling, 'the ones to beware of are Miss Carver, Morton Blake and William Stanchard – you know, the one with the ears. They are the ones who are watching us here. You can feel them in your head if you let them in. I know these things, my friend. It is in my blood, no? *Vive la Résistance!*'

He looked out of the window now. 'It is a beautiful evening. Come: I will show you a good tree for climbing.'

Liam sat high up in an evergreen oak, shiny, dark leaves all round him. Luc was higher up, just coming down from the very crown of the tree.

'I'm sorry,' said Liam.

Luc grinned. 'But you are still suspicious,' he said. 'That is fair. Shall I tell you? I thought you were a spy too. They don't like the way I come and go here. They would stop me if they could work out how to do it without damaging my gift! That afternoon, when you arrived, I thought that I might hear something interesting if I hid outside of the window.'

He shrugged. 'But no. Miss Carver knew I was there. I could feel her trying to get into my head. Like I say, she is one of the ones you should watch with care. She and Morton and William, they spy for Principal Willoughby. He likes to know exactly what is going on, I think. There may be others too . . . from outside. I think they are from the Lost Families or from the government. I don't think they trust our principal very far. No?'

After a long silence, Luc dropped on to a branch next to Liam's. 'My parents . . . you know?' he said. 'They gave up a great deal for me to come here. They made many sacrifices. They think it is a good thing for someone like you and like me. But I don't know. I am not so sure. I think they might have made a *big* mistake.'

17

A Telephone Call and an Intrusion

Never underestimate the importance of the human factor. Love, hate, jealousy, greed . . . they can intrude at any moment, disrupting even the best-laid plans.

First lesson of the morning was maths. Sitting in a classroom that had once been just an ordinary room in this house, the four of them paid attention as Mr Pullinger demonstrated calculus on the big screen.

It seemed so odd, sitting here in these surroundings, doing something as mundane as mathematics with fellow pupils who could read minds and move solid objects about without touching them.

Remembering Luc's warning, Liam was careful to guard his thoughts. They had talked about this in the night: how not to betray yourself in the presence of mind-spies like Anders Linley and Miss Carver.

'Always, you must concentrate,' Luc had urged. 'You feel them in your head, no? Push them away. Deflect them. Most of them, they find it very difficult, so if you push them away they just think they are having a bad day.'

Liam was not so confident of his abilities to push them

away. Luc's talent lay in his ability to deflect attention – maybe this made it easier for him to turn them away from his mind too.

Now, Liam was aware of the presences, the thought-shapes trying to intrude. Morton Blake was at the desk behind him, he knew, and Hayley and Briony were to his right. It was Morton he should watch, according to Luc. Liam concentrated on not thinking about certain subjects, and he concentrated on *deflecting*.

He concentrated on not thinking about the fact that he was even doing this, snuffing out thoughts and images as they occurred.

Calculus. That was his thing. That was what he allowed to fill his head.

Nothing else until he was free of this classroom, free of the building. He didn't dare think his own thoughts until there was some distance between him and all the prying minds.

At lunchbreak he made his excuses and went off for another of his walks. Time to relax. Time to let his guard drop a little and to think.

Hayley had taken to life in Senior House with gusto. It was as if she'd been waiting for this kind of recognition all the time she'd been in the main school, and now she was lapping it up. She seemed to have got to know everyone by their first names already, even Miss Carver and Mr Pullinger.

There was a hint of desperation in all this, Liam suspected: she was making the point that she was *here* and she *belonged*. Even so, he couldn't help but admire the way she took to it. He longed to be able to do something with that kind of open-eyed enthusiasm again, instead of suspecting everything, fearing everything.

This was never going to last, he realized.

He knew bad things had been done to his head. He knew that something terrible was going on and if he could only unlock his memories he might be able to work it all out.

Whatever . . . this could not go on.

Could he imagine lasting a whole year in this state of tension? A term? Even a month?

No. Something must give.

That left him with the choice: either sit back and watch carefully to see what would happen, or push it and see what gave first.

He didn't think he had ever been one to sit back and wait.

He sat on a grassy hummock behind the wall of what had once been the Senior House kitchen garden. He took his phone out and flipped it open.

There were no more strange messages, but the reminder was still there. He didn't know whether he'd set the reminder and forgotten or someone had planted it as some kind of prompt. Either way, it was there:

'13 June. Mum's birthday.'

That was today.

He closed his eyes and tried to remember, but nothing came. No memories of birthday cakes, no family parties.

Again, he wondered . . . this question had been plaguing him. How much of what was in his head was his own and how much had been put there, how much removed? Could they do that sort of thing to someone?

He thought of how much he had learned about the world in the last week and a half. So many strange things.

He could believe almost anything now.

He tapped a key on his phone to clear the screen saver. There was a number filed with the reminder. He thumbed the 'call' button and put the phone to his ear.

There was a pause of a second or two, then he heard the ringing tone. That, and the pounding of his pulse in his ears.

It rang three times, then there was a click, a silence, a woman's voice.

'Hello?'

He had hoped for – no, he had *expected* – a flash of recognition, triggered by that voice, but it did not come.

It was a soft voice, hesitant. Accentless, anonymous. He did not remember ever having heard this voice before.

'Hello?' the woman said again. 'Who is this?'

Liam swallowed. His throat felt paralysed. He managed to swallow again.

'Happy birthday,' he said, in little more than a whisper.

A long silence followed.

'Who . . .?' She started, stopped, then started again. 'Liam? That's you, isn't it? Liam? Oh my God. I thought we'd lost you. Liam, are you there?'

'Mum?' He closed his eyes, and that squeezed the first

of the tears out. 'Is that you, Mum? What's happening? What are they doing to me?'

'Liam. Are you okay? Where are you? Are you still at that place?'

He couldn't answer, couldn't say a thing through his choked-up throat.

'Liam. Listen to me. I don't know what you believe any more. I don't know what you remember and what they've brainwashed into you. Try to dig deep, Liam. Try to remember. Try to recover your true self. Do you understand?'

Sort of. 'I've been trying,' he said.

He gathered himself. 'Can we meet?' he asked. 'Can I see you?'

Another pause. 'Can you get out?'

'Maybe,' he told her. 'I think I know someone who could help.'

She was in Wolsey. *Just in case*, she had told him. So close!

They were going to meet tonight. They hadn't discussed what would happen after that, but Liam had no intention of coming back here. He would take the withdrawal symptoms and the long-term risks of abandoning the NATS medication.

Just one more afternoon of this madness and then he would be clear.

He stayed for a while on the hummock behind the old kitchen gardens, trying to gather himself. He mustn't give any of this away. He had to find that discipline again, the concentration he and Luc had discussed. One more afternoon of shutting out the prying minds of Morton Blake and Miss Carver and then he could relax.

But still, he had to hold it together all afternoon. He mustn't allow himself to slip now.

He headed back up to Senior House. He had an afternoon of English and history to get through. And he must find Luc.

He came to the house and went inside, still with ten minutes of the lunchbreak to go. He decided to head up to his room. Maybe Luc would be there.

Instead, on the landing, he met Mr Pullinger and Anders.

'Anders?' said Liam. 'What are *you* doing here?' Kids from the main school weren't allowed in Senior House ... Hayley had said he was jealous, but what could he be doing here now? What was he up to? Then he remembered Anders' role in NATS security and instantly clamped down on that thought, for fear of giving himself away.

'Connor,' said Mr Pullinger. 'Have you seen Hayley Warren?'

Hayley? Why were they looking for Hayley?

He thought of her room, then – just a brief, flashing thought, but it was enough.

'That way,' said Anders. 'Number six.' He gave Liam a dirty, aggressive look, then turned on his heel and strode along the corridor after Mr Pullinger.

'What . . .?'

They ignored him.

Mr Pullinger reached for the door and pushed it open.

'Hey! What's going on?'

She was in there, then. Liam felt guilty, as if he had

183

betrayed her by even thinking of her room. He hadn't known she was there. He'd only guessed.

Mr Pullinger was in the room and then Anders rushed in after him.

Liam followed them, stopping in the doorway.

Hayley was there in a T-shirt and jeans which she was struggling to fasten. She must have been changing. 'Mr Pullinger? *Anders?* What is it? Why are you just barging in like this? What's happened?' Then she looked past them to the doorway. 'Liam? What . . .?'

'Go back to your room, Liam. You weren't meant to see this.'

Liam turned and he saw Willoughby standing there in the corridor. Principal Willoughby was a good man. He radiated warmth, friendliness. Trustworthiness.

'Don't watch this, Liam. Go back to your room.'

Liam glanced over his shoulder. Hayley was cowering on her bed, hugging herself. She was frozen in place, her eyes locked on Mr Pullinger. She appeared unable to move, unable to speak any more.

Liam walked back along the corridor, past Principal Willoughby to the landing, and then along the opposite corridor to the room he shared with Luc.

He unlocked the door and went in.

He closed the door.

He walked across the room.

He lay down on the bed.

He slept.

18

In the Middle of the Night

You have to believe your own lies sometimes. Even if you only manage to do so for a short space of time. If you can fool yourself, it's far easier to fool the rest of the world.

Liam woke.

Someone was in the room with him.

Principal Willoughby. He was sitting on Luc's bed, leaning forward with his elbows on his knees, his hands clasped in front of him.

Liam felt good with Principal Willoughby in the room. This was the man who had identified his talent and moved him here to Senior House. This was a man who had Liam's best interests at heart.

Liam rubbed his eyes.

'What time is it? I should be in lessons.'

'It's all right, Connor,' said the principal. 'You have been excused for this afternoon. You had a traumatic experience. You saw an event you didn't fully understand.'

Liam remembered. He remembered seeing Anders and Mr Pullinger subduing Hayley in her room. 'Why?' he asked.

'Young Ms Warren had been up to no good,' said Principal Willoughby. 'It seems that she has been trying to sell her story to the national press. She wouldn't have got anywhere, of course. Who would believe a crank story about the secret existence of the Lost Families? And in any case, we have people in place to stop such things.'

Liam nodded. This explained her erratic behaviour. 'How did you find out?'

'Anders Linley discovered what she was up to. He reported it directly to me.'

Good old Anders. Liam had only shared the room with him for a week, but he missed his company. 'What will happen to her?'

'She has demonstrated her unworthiness. She was a threat to our security. Her talents will be neutralized and she will be returned to the outside world.'

That was good.

'Are you okay, Connor? We don't want you diverted from your course at such an early stage.'

'I'm okay,' said Liam. 'Just tired.'

He closed his eyes. Hayley had been stupid, but it was good that she was going to be taken care of.

He listened to the door closing, still thinking positive thoughts.

Hayley would be okay. Anders had done the right thing. He was glad that Principal Willoughby had taken the trouble to make sure he was okay – that just showed what a good place this was.

He thought along these lines for several minutes, until he was sure he was alone.

He thought these things because he had become very good at faking such thoughts now. Blocking his natural reactions and reshaping the thoughts into the kinds of things they would hope he would be thinking.

'So, let me get this straight, yes? This Anders has lied to them about Hayley because his jealousy is inflamed. They have taken her and . . . what is it that you fear? You are sure he was lying?'

Liam looked up at Luc. They were high up in the evergreen oak that Luc had shown him the previous day.

'Hayley was desperate to get into Senior House. She wouldn't have done anything to risk that, especially once she'd got here. She told me Anders was mad that the two of us had moved here and left him behind. You should have seen him when they came for her. He was gloating. He'd won. He thought he'd been dumped, so this was his revenge.'

'But what will they do?'

'I don't know.' But it was bad. He had had another of those memory flashes when Willoughby had been talking to him, a vivid flashback that he had suppressed instantly. Kath, in Norwich, guzzling pills from a plastic container. And another: something medical, something that called out to a fear rooted deep down in his mind. He touched his implant scar. 'They'll take this, for a start. They'll kill off the spark. Who knows *how* she might end up?'

'So what do we do?'

'What *can* we do? We're powerless.' Until this moment

he had clung to the idea that they might be able to help Hayley, but no . . .

Luc climbed higher in the tree again. He seemed to like pushing it to its limit, climbing out along the slimmest of branches that you'd swear would not take his weight. When he came back down again a few minutes later, Liam caught his eye.

'Luc,' he said.

'Yes?'

'There *was* one other thing . . .'

It was dark, with clouds covering the stars and the moon.

Liam perched on the window ledge. When Luc did this he just took his weight on his hands and swung out from here, but now that Liam was in this position he couldn't quite work out how he did it. Instead, he turned awkwardly and reached out with his right hand.

He found the iron pipe and stretched his right foot out too, until it struck the pipe. It felt solid enough. He took his weight on the right side and swung round, grabbing the pipe with his left hand, just as he started to slide with his feet. He did as Luc had told him, leaning back so that he pulled out with his hands, which drove his feet in against the wall and stopped them from skidding. Slowly, he edged his way down.

Luc clapped a hand on his shoulder when they both stood on the ground. Silently, they slipped away into the trees. Liam's eyes had adjusted now, but he still found it hard to see where he was placing his feet and he stumbled several times.

They crossed the playing field.

'So,' said Liam, finally breaking their silence with a low whisper, 'how do we get to Wolsey?'

'Come,' said Luc. 'You will see.'

They skirted round the main schoolhouse until they came to one of the outbuildings. Luc leaned close to a side door and then stood back as it swung open.

Inside, he produced a penlight torch and flashed its narrow beam around. They were in a garage. There was a big blue car there, surrounded by tools and boxes and heaped bags.

'Here,' said Luc, handing Liam the torch. 'You open the door on the right, yes? There is a bolt at top and bottom, and one in the middle.'

Liam took the torch and went to the front of the building. It was just as Luc described. He slid the bolts and swung the door open. Behind him, a car engine sprung into life.

It sounded so loud!

He hurried back and scrambled in through the passenger door that Luc had opened.

Luc was beaming at him. 'You British . . .' he said. 'Everything is on the wrong side, but I am okay. Now. Let me see. The accelerator.'

The car revved and lurched forward, just missing the door as it swung out on to the gravel.

'Oh no,' said Luc. 'Gears! My father . . . we have an automatic, you know. It makes things simpler.'

They stopped and Liam jumped out to swing the garage door shut, then he was back in the car and they were revving down the long drive in a gear far too low.

Fearfully, Liam peered back through the rear windscreen and side windows, but there was no sign of lights going on in the school building, no dark figures hurrying outside. At the end of the drive, they turned right on to the Wolsey road.

'Okay,' said Luc, having mastered crunching into a higher gear quite quickly, 'there must be lights on this thing, no?'

'You are sure, my friend?'

Liam nodded. 'I'm not going back there,' he said. 'Whatever happens.'

Luc shrugged. 'Okay. It has been good knowing you. I mean that, you know?'

Liam felt bad about abandoning Luc to return on his own. He felt bad about not telling him the entire truth too. He had just told him he had a friend here, but hadn't said that it was his mother. 'Look out for Hayley if you get the chance,' he said.

Luc shrugged again. 'I climb trees and steal cars and get away with a lot of things they don't know how to stop,' he said. 'But I think that miracles are maybe a bit beyond my abilities, no?'

Liam stood back and watched as the car set off into the night.

He retreated into the shadows and flipped open his phone.

She answered on the second ring. 'Hello?'

'I'm here,' he said. 'In Wolsey. Where are you?'

'Okay. You know the seafront? The Golden Anchor chip

shop? Opposite, at the top of the beach, there's a shelter. It looks out towards the sea. You know the one?'

'I'll find it.' He had never been to Wolsey. Not in the memories he could reach. Before, though. He thought he had been here before.

He was in an area where the High Street opened out, with angled parking spaces lined up like herringbones along the central area. Shops crammed either side of the street, the brightly painted buildings jostling, as if squeezed into too little space.

She didn't trust him, he realized. That was why she was meeting him out here and not wherever she was staying. She had told him very little. She was giving him no information that he might betray to anyone reading his mind.

That was sensible, he supposed. He had done exactly the same thing with Luc just now.

Trust had to be earned.

He took one of the small side roads, away from the High Street. Judging by the way the road had come in, he had worked out that the sea must lie in this direction.

It did. He came to a road that ran parallel to the High Street. On one side there were more of the higgledy-piggledy, brightly coloured town houses, while on the other a concrete sea-defence wall held back a bank of shingle at the top of the beach.

He looked left and then right.

There: a dark shape on the beach. That must be the shelter.

He walked in that direction and soon saw that he had been right: the chip shop, the Golden Anchor, lay in darkness on his side of the road.

He crossed. It was funny. Only a week and a half ago he had walked into NATS, starting a new life. So much had happened in a short time, and here he was, leaving all that behind. He was not going back.

He was scared, he realized. Would he recognize her? She had been blocked out of his mind so successfully that parts of his brain still thought of her as dead.

Steps led up the wall.

He climbed to the top, then down on to the shingle on the other side.

His steps crunched with each footfall, and he saw movement in the shelter, a figure coming out to greet him. She came out of the darkness, and he saw her, and recognized her. It was Kath.

19

Nowhere to Run to, Nowhere to Hide

Some people believe that history is a kind of force, a thing with its own momentum. They argue that the major events of history – or at least, events very similar and with the same result – would happen regardless of who is around to take part: history happens because the world is ready for it.

Others argue that history is shaped by key figures: that without Leonardo, Napoleon, Darwin and Hitler the world would be a very different place today. Some people cling to this belief with an almost religious fervour.

It might be their only source of hope.

'Hello, Liam.'

Kath. He stared at her and she flinched, raising a hand to her head.

'Whew . . . You're hot, aren't you? Intense. What have they been doing to you?'

He remembered the pills she took. How she had struggled before . . . some time in the past . . . with having him close.

She walked beyond him and climbed the steps set against the wall. 'Come on,' she said. 'I feel exposed out here. You never know when they're watching.'

He hurried after her as she turned left along the road behind the wall.

'It's not what you were expecting,' she said. 'I'm sorry. What are you going to do now?'

He thought of his dreams of only a few minutes before. Of finding his mother and setting off for a new life somewhere.

'I have a friend,' he said finally. 'She's in trouble. I want to help her, and then I just want to get out of all this. How do I do that, Kath? How do I break free?'

She didn't answer. He suspected she didn't *have* an answer.

The road emerged from behind the wall and cut through the shingle at the head of Wolsey Point. Ahead of them, there was a row of white cottages set at an angle across the beach.

'I'm staying here,' said Kath. 'With some friends. They're out now. We have the place to ourselves. We can talk for a time.'

He followed her to number three and waited as she unlocked the door. They went through to the kitchen and she set the kettle on an electric ring to heat. He had been here before, he knew.

They sat at a long, narrow table.

'I'm sorry, Liam.' She wouldn't meet his eyes. Instead, she stared down at the table's surface. 'I'm not your aunt. Is that what you remember me as? I lose track. I'm not your sister, either. Or your mother. I've played all those roles at times. Somewhere in your head you have me in some kind of merged role as the older woman in your life, I suppose. They suck you in. Trap you. Sometimes I even forget who I am myself . . .'

'I thought I was coming here to meet my mother.'

She glanced at him for an instant, then looked away. 'You never had a mother, Liam. Or if there ever was anyone who played that role in your life, then it was a long time ago and your memories are probably so mangled there's no knowing the truth. I'm sorry, Liam. I . . .'

She glanced at him again.

'Where did you get my number?' she asked, breaking a long silence. 'That threw me.'

He took out his phone and flashed the little screen at her. 'On here,' he said flatly. 'A reminder.'

She nodded. 'They must have overlooked that.'

'What's this all about?'

Kath suddenly looked intense. 'All around the world,' she said, 'our kind are enslaved. They keep us in military bases or big commercial research units; they call us analysts and facilitators, but really we're trapped, like battery hens or laboratory rats. They watch us, sort through us, and use us. They hook us to drugs that let us use our gifts and maybe even live a few years longer, even though those same drugs are just as likely to kill us young. They use us, control us and destroy us. That's how it has always been.'

She went to the kettle, which was whistling on the hob. 'In theory, NATS is part of that system, but in reality Sir

Peter is running it like his own little kingdom – with *our* interests in mind. He wants to free us. The implants: they think they're just part of the enslavement, but in reality Sir Peter hopes that they will be a lot safer than the drug programmes and let us live longer.'

'Why me? What are they doing to me?'

She sat again, having taken the kettle off the heat. 'Talent is very variable. Unpredictable. Some people only have a touch of it. Lots of those who have it find that it fades in adulthood – that's one of the reasons places like NATS are so important: they like to start using us as early as possible. With some people it emerges late and gets steadily stronger. Every so often, maybe once in a generation or even less, someone special emerges.

'The normal world uses us, but they're scared of us too, Liam! They don't want any of us to become too powerful, so they watch for any with special gifts. They're looking out for anyone who might be special enough to pull the Lost together, someone who might channel their powers into something far more potent. Someone who could lead us to freedom.'

Liam stared at her, the intensity in her eyes. She scared him now. Where before she had just been a sad, broken figure, now she truly scared him.

'They think that's me?' he said, appalled.

She sat back and looked him in the eye. 'You have the right talent,' she said. 'And it appears to be pretty potent. It's still unlikely,' she concluded, 'but you've passed all the tests so far. Sir Peter thinks he can shock it out of you: he reckons terror can accelerate the emergence of talents like yours. The harder he pushes, the more your capabilities will grow.'

He shook his head. It was preposterous.

'Don't dismiss it, Liam. Don't ever do that. The government would eliminate people like you: people who might be a threat to the way things are.'

'Isn't that a bit drastic?'

'You want drastic?' she said. 'Like I said, these special talents only come along rarely, but the government agencies who control us are terrified that it might happen again. They exploit our talents, but they don't want us getting too strong. They'll go to any lengths to stop that happening. The nuclear bombs in Hiroshima and Nagasaki in the Second World War? They were targeted on a young woman who many thought might be one of the special ones. The Great Fire of London? A similar story: a young boy, this time. Usually it's less extreme: a bullet, some poison, a car crash. You're lucky. You really are lucky that Sir Peter is on your side and hasn't just quietly swept you away.'

Liam struggled to think. No matter how hard he tried, he couldn't see Sir Peter Willoughby as being on his side. It was just a different slavemaster . . .

There was a sound from the front of the house, a rattle of a key in the lock, the door opening, voices.

Kath looked up past Liam. 'That'll be them,' she said. 'I'm sorry, Liam. You really have been like a brother to me sometimes. You won't remember, but there have been good times too. They keep wiping you and starting again. Writing and rewriting to try to shape you, mould you. I've begged them to leave you alone, but . . .'

This woman, whoever she was . . . looked broken, defeated.

He leaned across the table. 'Kath, tell me,' he said. She looked up now, meeting his gaze. 'Where is my real mother? What happened to her?'

She shook her head. 'I don't know,' she told him. 'I'm sorry. I don't know. But maybe *you* know. If you can dig deep enough.'

Liam turned as a man came into the room. He was wearing a dark suit and he had thinning grey hair and dark-framed glasses.

'Liam,' said the man in a gentle Scottish accent. 'You won't remember me. Or my two friends.' He waved a hand at two men who had followed him in. 'Mr Smith and Mr Smith. They're not related.'

But Liam did remember. He remembered these cottages, and he remembered this man. He had helped him once before. Maybe all was not lost.

'Oh, Liam, I think you'll find that it is,' said this man whom he had once known as Alastair.

He was a mind-spy, then. And an enemy.

'Oh, Liam. How juvenile to divide the world up along such strict lines! Surely we are all working for the greater good. We just adopt different strategies. I was a sceptic, you know. I really didn't think Sir Peter was right about you. But you should be grateful. If Sir Peter and I had been doing our jobs, you would have been eliminated a long time ago. The authorities don't want him taking any risks. But he convinced me to join him and we gave you a chance. We nurtured you. We established all the best conditions to help your gift emerge. We think you may be a very rare individual, Liam.'

'Someone special.'

Alastair nodded.

'Well, you can tell Willoughby he's mistaken,' said Liam. He felt certain of that. He was just an ordinary fifteen-year-old caught up in a world most people didn't even know existed.

'Oh yes?' said Alastair. 'How would *you* know?'

'Okay,' said Alastair, gathering up an attaché case from a work surface. 'Time to go.'

Liam didn't need to ask where.

He projected resigned thoughts. He wondered if he had been wrong about Willoughby – *Sir Peter*, as these people called him. If he really had protected Liam from the authorities then maybe he deserved a chance.

He followed Alastair through the house and was followed in turn by the two Mr Smiths.

He would do what they asked. That's what they wanted him to think.

They crossed the shingle to the road and waited while one Mr Smith went round to the side of the house to start the car.

Liam sprinted.

He had trainers on and he was young. They had suits and shoes that wouldn't help them run. He had a chance.

'Hey!' That was Alastair.

He glanced back. The other Smith was chasing him, but Alastair just stood there, fumbling with his case.

A multicoloured flash smothered Liam's senses. It seemed to have started somewhere inside his head.

He felt nothing, heard nothing, saw nothing.

He was on the ground, gasping for air.

He looked up and Alastair came into view. He had his little notebook computer balanced on the palm of one hand. 'Please, Liam,' he said. 'You're being disrespectful. We are professionals, you know. We are in control. Your implant isn't just there for *your* benefit. It was specially built for you. It gives us extra options, like –' He tapped a key with a flourish and Liam saw another flash of light, weaker and briefer this time.

When he opened his eyes again, Alastair was squatting, leaning forward on one hand so that he was close to Liam's face, peering at him sideways. 'Come on, Liam,' he said. 'You're a bright lad. Did you ever think, even for one moment, that you have been beyond our reach? Did you ever think you had slipped away from our control?'

20

Somewhere Deep

It was like a Russian doll: pull it apart and you find another slightly smaller doll inside. And inside that another. With Liam, it was the other way around: he was on the inside and it felt as if he was surrounded by layer upon layer upon layer. Every time he broke out . . . another layer.

But what if he turned the other way? What if he dug deeper?

They bundled him into the back of a big white car. Alastair drove, and Liam slumped in the back with a Mr Smith on either side of him. He felt thought-shapes pressing in on his mind and he pushed them away angrily.

'Easy, easy,' said Alastair, looking back over his shoulder. 'No point fighting it now, lad.'

Kath stood in the doorway of number three, her face almost as pale as the whitewashed walls of the cottages. She didn't wave, just watched as the car headed off along the road through the banked shingle.

Liam drifted in and out of consciousness as the car threaded its way through the narrow streets of Wolsey and out on to the Suffolk back roads. 'You'll feel a little rough,' said Alastair conversationally. 'Your implant induced a mild seizure, a short-circuiting of the nerves in your brain. It's not something we'd want to have to do to you too often, you know.'

These were the people Liam was lucky to have on his side, as they had told him . . .

He recognized the drive at NATS: long and straight, lined by tall poplar trees. As the car pulled up in the gravelled semicircle before the main building, Liam peered round to the side where the outhouses were. The garage door was closed and there was no sign of Luc. But then there wouldn't be, he realized, given the nature of Luc's ability to avoid being noticed.

He was clutching at straws.

They led him inside. They weren't returning him to Senior House, then. He wondered what lay in store for him here.

A room. Much like any other pupil's room, except that it was a single, not shared.

There was a bed up against one wall and a desk and wardrobe opposite. At the far end, opposite the door, there was a tall sash window. He went to it and saw that it was screwed down from the outside.

So it was a room much like any other, except that it had a screwed-down window and a door that had been locked behind him.

A room much like a prison cell, then.

He wondered if Hayley might be nearby, locked up in a similar room to this one.

Perhaps, if they had not dealt with her already.

It came as something of a shock to him to realize that it had only been earlier today – or yesterday, as he was sure it must be past midnight now – that Hayley had been taken from Senior House. Only a matter of hours.

Perhaps she *was* nearby, then.

The thought didn't cheer him. What could he do?

He sat in the chair at the desk.

He remembered Kath – if that was really her name. He remembered what she had told him.

Maybe you know. If you can dig deep enough.

She had talked about what was happening to him as if it was some kind of repeated cycle. Trial and error. They kept wiping him and starting again, trying to mould him, to shape him into this legendary figure who would solve everyone's problems, unite the Lost Families and lead them to freedom.

He had protected some of his old memories once. Memories from *before*. The gull, the children singing, Three Trunker, the coastguards' cottages . . .

Those memories had mattered to him, and he had clung to them through whatever Willoughby and his people had done. The gull: freedom, from when he had broken free once before. The children singing: his father betraying him. Three Trunker: a place of friendship. The cottages: Alastair, and help.

He had been wrong in three of these, he realized. He had never been free. Anders, the mind-spy, had been one of the friends with whom he had shared Three Trunker. And Alastair had betrayed him too, just like his father.

But they had been memories that he had managed to

hang on to and rediscovered when they should have been lost to him.

What if there were other memories buried deeper? Memories from some earlier stage in this cycle of moulding and remoulding him. Memories are who you are. You hold on to them with all you have.

He tried and tried but nothing would come. He kept on though, it was all he had.

And finally, it came to him some time in the depths of the night, in that dead time before dawn starts to silver the sky.

'You don't have to do this, Liam. You don't have to go through with this.'

His father held him by the shoulders so that he had to look back into his father's eyes.

Slowly, Liam nodded. He'd had enough. The mind games, the playing with his head.

He was twelve years old, and he had just learned that the things Dad and Sir Peter had been telling him weren't true. He'd had enough of the lies.

'I want to know what happened to Mum,' he said patiently, as if he was talking to a small child. 'I want to know. What really happened.'

His father nodded. 'Okay, son.'

They were out on the Point. They had driven down here from Wolsey in Dad's old Land Rover, through the high gates in the first fence, through the gap in the second fence, and through the gates in the final fence. Here, to the old camp.

Now his father started the Land Rover up again and they drove on past the big hangar to a cluster of buildings. The windows and doors were boarded up and tamarisk and gorse grew all around, leaving only narrow trails through to the buildings themselves.

A yellow sign read, 'Danger! Contaminated premises.'

They left the car there and walked through to the second of the four buildings. The board over the door lifted aside easily and they went through. There was a door in the rear wall. Liam's father opened it and they stepped into a small lift.

'You realize Doctor Shastri is going to have to edit your memories of all this, don't you?' Liam's father pointed out.

Liam nodded. He wanted to *know*, even if only for a short time.

Then his father leaned close. 'You have to work really hard to hang on to memories when Doctor Shastri removes them.' And he winked.

They stepped out of the lift and into a long, brightly lit corridor, much longer than the building above them.

'So, Dad,' said Liam, 'are you going to tell me?'

'Give it time,' his father told him. 'Now you're down here, you might as well see some of what's here among Sir Peter's Follies.'

Liam looked at his father. His guard seemed to have slipped this afternoon, perhaps because he knew that these memories would be wiped soon.

They went into a room full of glass display cabinets and framed photographs, mostly of small children. In the cabinets were foetuses – all damaged, deformed. One even had two heads: one normal, the second stunted like a doll's head, sticking out at a strange angle.

Liam stared.

'Sir Peter's failed experiments,' said his father. 'Are you okay?'

Liam nodded and backed out of the room. He came to lean against the wall opposite the door, out in the bright corridor. His father stood in the doorway.

'He comes down here sometimes,' he said. 'Sir Peter. He comes down here to remind himself of the cost of his grand project. That's what he claims. I'm not so sure, myself. I think he comes down here to gloat at the power he has over us all, his power over creation.'

'The pictures?'

The pictures on the wall . . . He recognized one. He had seen a smaller version of it before, framed. This larger version had been cropped closely round the small boy's head and shoulders, but in the smaller version you could see the boy, held up in his father's arms.

Liam stared at his own father. 'Why is there a picture of me in there?'

'He thinks you're his success, Liam. Finally. He thinks you're going to be something quite extraordinary.'

His father stepped across to him and put a hand on his shoulder. 'Come on, we'll go now. You've seen too much. I should never have brought you here.'

Liam resisted the pressure on his shoulder. 'No,' he said. 'You were going to . . . my mother?'

★

They passed rooms. The doors had one-way viewing panels set into them, so that they could look in. There were people inside. People of a variety of ages, some with tubes sticking out of noses, mouths and arms, others just sitting in easy chairs, staring at flickering pictures on their TVs.

'It's a nursing home, I suppose,' said Liam's father.

'Are they all . . .?'

'No. They're not all survivors of Sir Peter's experiments, although some of them are. Some are just survivors of our condition.'

They came to a door and stopped. An old woman was inside, staring at her television.

Instead of moving on, Liam's father reached for the door handle and pushed. They went in, but the old woman didn't acknowledge their arrival.

'She's quite oblivious,' he said. 'One consequence of our condition is that we can be afflicted by any number of damaging illnesses when we reach middle age. She's only forty-seven, believe it or not, but she doesn't have long left now. The drugs hold it off for a time, but they're addictive, which is another hold those in power have over the Lost Families. We're starting to break free from the drugs with the implants, but the technology is new. Who knows, Liam: maybe one day you'll have an implant.

'Sir Peter has been running a breeding programme,' Liam's father went on to explain. 'Finding the purest blood-lines of the Lost Families and matching them up in the hope that we will breed true again. If our blood is pure, we will be stronger. And if our blood is pure, there's a greater chance that those with really special gifts will emerge – talents that will pull us together and help us break free and emerge from the shadows of the talentless masses. When the breeding programme identifies someone with particularly pure blood, they breed from them over and over again. If it's a woman, they harvest her eggs and implant them in other women who will carry them.'

He raised a hand, waving towards the old woman. 'Liam, you've never had a real mother, as such. Not in the way that other people have. But . . . well . . . meet your biological mother.'

Liam stared, just as the old woman stared at the screen. She wasn't seeing the pictures, wasn't hearing the sound. In most senses, she was hardly there at all.

In the lift back to the surface, Liam's father said, 'I'm sorry. You really shouldn't have seen that. I'll talk to Doctor Shastri as soon as we're back. We'll sort out your memories.'

Liam nodded. He was glad he had seen it. It had made a big impression on him. A deep impression. One he would hang on to.

Because one day he would put a stop to Sir Peter's awful experiments.

21

The Here and Now

It usually pays to be rational and cautious. Assess a situation, weigh up the pros and cons, and then make your decision.

But sometimes you can't be sure.

Sometimes you can only weigh up the likelihoods and the vague possibilities.

Sometimes the most rational course of action is to take the plunge.

Willoughby came to see him. He had Liam's father with him.

Liam remembered Alastair's words of the night before. Sir Peter had protected Liam. He was working for the good of the Lost Families. And his father – what was his role in all this now? Liam deliberately muddled up his thoughts, projecting *confused*, and *hoping Alastair was right about these people*, and similar sentiments.

Willoughby stared at him, so that Liam felt like an insect pinned down on a board, being studied through a magnifying lens.

'You've been a lot of trouble,' said the principal. 'I'm

inclined to terminate our experiment. It would be easy to neutralize you, just as we're going to do with your little friend. Snuff out your spark.'

Normality, Liam thought. Was he being offered normality?

'But your father, here, has persuaded me that we should give you another chance, Connor. He proposes that we should work with you on a more equal basis. No more song and dance. We have seen your gift develop dramatically through the testing process, but now, perhaps, we should move on. Work with me on my project, Connor, and together we can lead the Lost Families out into the open! Freedom for our kind.'

Liam suppressed thoughts of the failed experiments out at the camp. He suppressed the thought that he was staring into the eyes of an absolute madman.

He raised a hand to his head.

'I . . .' he said, and stopped. He thought of confusion, of blinding colours flashing across his senses, of pain in his implant. Last night. This had happened to him last night, and it still hurt, still left him reeling.

Willoughby glanced at Liam's father. 'Come on,' he said. 'He's still recovering from the seizure. I *told* Al not to damage him! We've invested a lot in this project.'

Liam's father nodded. 'We'll give him a bit longer.' He turned as they left the room and said, 'Liam, when you're ready to talk – ask for me, okay?'

Liam struggled to think whether he was really being offered a way out, or if he was just being drawn in ever deeper.

Work with Willoughby? How could he ever work with that mad tyrant?

But the alternative was to let them do whatever they had to do in order to neutralize his gift. The easiest way would be to kill him, but Willoughby had implied that they hadn't dealt with Hayley yet, so Liam suspected that something more elaborate than murder was involved.

Was this a way out, then? Let them do what they wanted . . .

If he really was so powerful – one of these special ones they talked about – then maybe he should let them contain him. Control him for the good of everyone.

Perhaps.

He stood at the window. He was high up in the main NATS building. Just a figure in a distant window to anyone who might happen to glance up and see him.

For a moment, he considered trying to mark the letters H–E–L–P on the window somehow, but even if someone saw it, they would only go to Reception, or to one of the teachers. That wouldn't get him far at all.

He remembered Luc's claim that there were spies from outside agencies here, as well as Sir Peter's people. But even if Liam could somehow contact one of these people, why would he ever trust them to be on his side?

He wondered what Hayley must be going through. She had just been given the place in Senior House she had always wanted and then had it snatched away from her. He somehow doubted they would have bothered to explain too much to her about what was going on, and what they did tell her of Anders' lies was probably just hopelessly confusing.

Maybe he could strike some kind of deal? If he was willing to work with Willoughby, maybe he could convince them that Anders had been lying, and they should give Hayley another chance too?

He spent a long time running through the options in his head. Finally, he banged on his door and asked to see his father.

A few minutes later, the door opened and his father stepped in.

Liam stood by the window. His father looked at him, squinting against the afternoon sunlight. He looked nervous, shifty.

'So,' his father said, 'how are you feeling now?'

Liam tried to sense whether there was anything going on, any thought-shapes probing his mind. Nothing. He shrugged. 'A lot clearer, I think.'

'Good. Good.'

Liam stared at his father and wondered why it was that he had taken him to see Sir Peter's Follies that time. Was he sowing the seeds of rebellion, or was he just playing his part, raising the levels of trauma as they tried to force Liam's gifts to emerge? And why had he hinted that Liam might be able to hang on to his memories, even when they tried to wipe them?

London's burning, London's burning. Fire! Fire! Fire! Fire!

'What's going on, Dad? What are you up to?'

He hadn't expected that. He looked away, to the side, down at his feet. Then he looked back up at Liam and met his eyes. 'This is really happening, son,' he said. 'We're in the here and now. It's not another remixed memory. It's not something from the past that you're only now managing to remember. It's not a fake episode implanted into your head to try to shape you into the person *he* wants. This is *now*. What you do is real. The decisions you make are real. This isn't a game. Sir Peter never plays games. Do you understand?'

Liam nodded. He had no past, or at least no past that he could be sure of. And he didn't know where the future lay. All he *had* was the here and now.

'Tell me,' he said. 'How do I *know*? How do I know you're even my father?'

The man across the room shook his head. 'You don't,' he told Liam. 'I can tell you that you are, because that's the truth, but how can you ever know anything's true? Things are never what they seem.'

That phrase . . . Liam recognized it. The message on his phone. 'You've been nudging me along, haven't you? Helping me piece things together . . .'

His father shrugged. 'All I ask is that you judge me by my actions.'

'But . . .' But his father had betrayed him. Liam couldn't remember the details but he knew that to be true. And now . . . now when this conversation was over, his father would walk out of that door leaving Liam still a prisoner.

'I've made some tough decisions,' his father told him now. 'I have a lot on my conscience. But I've always looked out for you, Liam. I've always tried to keep you close, so that I can make sure you're safe. And sometimes I've had to do things I never wanted to do. But I've always tried to do what's *right*. Do you understand?'

There was a long silence between them.

'So what next?' Liam finally asked. 'What do you want me to do?'

His father shook his head. 'I can't say, son. It's not my choice. It's yours. It's up to you.'

Liam stared at him. It was the first time anyone had said that to him.

That was when he decided for sure. A plan of action.

'Will you do something for me?' he asked his father. 'Will you tell Luc Renaudier where I am?'

His father nodded.

'And there's something else,' said Liam. 'You people – you're scared of me, aren't you? Even you, of all people. You don't know what I might become and that terrifies you.'

His father didn't object, which was answer enough.

'There's something else,' said Liam. 'I want you to do something else for me too.'

22

Unless You Can Think of Anything Better . . .

Those Russian dolls again. One lesson they should teach you is that you should persevere: keep on chipping away and one day you will reach the final layer.

One day.

Liam lay back on the bed in his locked-up, screwed-down room. He wondered if he had made the right call. Had his father really done as he asked or was he, even now, having a good laugh about it with Willoughby and Alastair?

The young fool! He still doesn't understand. He can never win. No one will ever be on his side. We're going to have to carry on teaching him that lesson until he gets it.

He rubbed at his implant scar and remembered the flashing colours. His head ached – a quiet, deep pulse. He wondered what he had in there. What gift? Something about making people strong, Miss Carver had said. Was he really one of these legendary figures? He just felt the same as he always had, but then, how would he know?

Sometime, much later, he was dozing, catching up on some of the sleep he had missed.

'Are you there, Liam?'

He knew that voice, that accent, but he couldn't quite place it.

'It is me, Luc Renaudier. Your room buddy. Are you there, Liam? I am trying to reach you.'

Liam sat up, shaking his head. Was Luc projecting his voice at him somehow? Communicating directly into his head? The voice sounded hollow, disembodied.

'Liam. Answer me.'

He thought hard, trying to project an answer.

'Liam. Please tell me that I am right and that I am not now making a dangerous fool of myself.'

He looked up. The voice wasn't in his head. It was in his ceiling!

'Luc?' he said. He stood on the bed so his head was close to the ceiling. 'Luc? Are you up there?'

'Ah, that is good. I did not think I had got it wrong. I told you I am good at all this, no?'

Liam dropped to the floor and peered up. The ceiling was solid. No air ducts, no ventilation panels. Solid plaster.

He heard a scratching sound.

A short time later, a flake of plaster came away from the ceiling and a metal blade poked through: a screwdriver. It waggled from side to side, widening its hole, and then slid back up.

A hacksaw blade replaced it and started to saw a wavery line across the ceiling.

Liam watched the line grow, curling back on itself in a rough oval. He kept glancing at the door, fearing that someone would come for him at any moment.

'Prepare to catch,' said Luc, as the oval was almost complete.

Liam stood beneath the panel and there was a soft thud over his head. Luc must be trying to stamp the plaster through. Another thud, and the oval block came away and fell into Liam's waiting arms, accompanied by a shower of dust and other debris from the ceiling space.

He staggered back, dropping the plaster on the bed and waving at the air round his face to clear it of the dust.

He looked up and saw his old room-mate beaming back down at him.

'It is not the most elegant of escape methods,' Luc said. 'But . . . unless you can think of anything better?'

Luc had come prepared. As he so often pointed out, he was really rather good at this sort of thing. He lowered a knotted rope into the room. 'It is okay,' he said. 'I have secured it to a beam. You just need to climb.'

Liam grabbed the rope and pulled his weight clear of the ground. As soon as he tried to put his feet on the rope, his body swung wildly and he had to drop to the floor again.

'Calmer,' said Luc. 'It is a rope, not a drainpipe.'

Liam grabbed the rope again and this time took his weight on his arms and pulled straight up. It was hard work, but when his feet found the rope and slid down to rest on a knot, he could ease the strain for a moment. He reached up and pulled himself higher. The rope swung, but not nearly as wildly as before.

As his shoulders squeezed through the gap, he felt Luc's hands under his arms, pulling.

He grabbed a beam, and hauled himself through, struggling as his legs caught on the plaster lip.

It was dark in the ceiling space. Light came up through the hole Luc had cut and through joins in the roof above, but not enough to see clearly by.

'Thank you,' said Liam. 'I was just beginning to run out of ideas, myself . . .' He pulled the rope back up through the gap. 'We have to get Hayley,' he said. 'Last I heard they hadn't touched her, but it can't be long.'

In the gloom, Luc nodded. He had his penlight torch. He took it from a shirt pocket and flashed it beyond Liam. 'That way,' he said. 'They have Hayley there. I have already spoken to her. She is waiting.'

'How will we get out? Do you have any ideas?'

Luc grinned, his teeth flashing white in the near darkness. 'Don't worry, my friend. I have prepared for that.'

There were wooden beams everywhere. They moved carefully along inside the roof, treading only on the joists and clambering over and under beams that thrust up at angles between ceiling and roof.

Luc led the way, and soon he stopped and squatted. There was a chalk mark on the joist before him. He turned to Liam and, shining his torch at his own face, put a finger up to his lips to indicate silence. He ducked down and put his head into the gap between two joists.

He must have made a hole, Liam realized.

'Hayley!' Luc hissed. 'It is me again. Luc. I have Liam with me now.'

The way must be clear then.

Liam watched as Luc withdrew the hacksaw blade from

his shirt pocket and began to saw again, holding one end of the blade wrapped up in a handkerchief.

A few minutes later, he was through. There was muffled coughing from the room below and Liam saw Hayley through the hole, staggering away with a panel of plaster in her arms, spluttering in the dust.

Liam had been carrying the rope and now he handed it to Luc and watched as his friend secured it round a beam with a deft knot. They lowered the other end into the room.

'Okay, Hayley. You need to climb, yes?'

She caught the rope and pulled, testing its strength. She peered up into the opening. 'I . . .' She hesitated. Her face was pale and her eyes were brimming with tears. 'You two go on,' she told them. 'Okay? They said they'd treat me so that things were better. I'll be okay.'

'They'll kill a part of your brain, Hayley,' said Liam. 'That's what they mean by "treatment".'

She sucked on her lower lip and looked away.

'She's scared,' Liam whispered to Luc, suddenly understanding. Her worst fears: rats, spiders . . . creatures of the dark, dusty corners of old buildings! 'She has intense fears – phobias. I'll go down there and talk to her. Okay?'

Luc nodded.

Liam took the rope and shinned down it into the room.

Hayley stared at him, tears on her face. 'I'm sorry, Liam, but I can't. My arms and legs. They're just jelly. I can't go up there.'

'It's okay,' said Liam. 'I know what's bothering you. But it's the only way out. It's fine up there. Luc and I have

219

been up there and it's just dust and electric cables. That's all. You have to come with us, Hayley. You can't let them mess with your brain.'

She was shaking her head. 'You don't understand,' she said. 'I can't do it. I can't go up there, with all those . . .' She shuddered and turned her head away from him.

'You have to confront your fears,' Liam said. 'Think of your talent, your gift. You can turn your fears into your greatest strength. You can beat them.'

She met his eyes again. He was winning. She was going to have a go.

'Luc's up there now. I'll come up the rope behind you. We won't be up there long and then we'll be free. You can beat it, Hayley. Okay?'

Just then, they heard someone outside in the corridor.

Liam raised a finger to his lips, hoping the footsteps would carry on past the door. He gestured at the hole in the ceiling and, after another long pause, Hayley nodded and reached for the rope.

The footsteps halted outside.

There was a rattle at the door, a key in the lock, and the handle turned.

Liam darted behind the door just as it swung open. Hayley stood in front of the knotted rope, as if somehow she might hide it. She stared at whoever was in the doorway, then . . . glanced at Liam. Immediately, the door half shut and Liam saw Principal Willoughby with one of the Mr Smiths at his shoulder. Briefly, the principal looked surprised, then he caught himself, composed his features, and shook his head slowly.

'Really,' he said. 'I had hoped for so much more.'

They stood for a few seconds in silence.

Liam smothered any thoughts of Luc up in the roof space, and hoped Hayley had been quick-witted enough to do the same. If they didn't know Luc was there, maybe he would be able to come up with something.

Willoughby looked at Liam. 'It looks to me as if you have made your decision, Connor. It is a shame that we won't be able to continue our experiment. You really were doing rather well. I thought you might be a significant figure in the future of our kind.' He glanced at Mr Smith, smiling. 'Instead . . . another of Sir Peter's Follies, eh?'

They both laughed.

Liam looked at Hayley.

She looked mad. She looked furious. And she was looking right at Sir Peter Willoughby.

He seemed to sense something. He stopped laughing and met her look, an eyebrow raised.

Something was happening. Liam had a sudden memory flash of a session in the psiLab over at Wolsey Camp. Hayley was focusing her fears, projecting them.

A spider the size of Liam's fist appeared on Willoughby's left cheek. It had thick, bristly legs and a fat, bulbous body.

Willoughby barely flinched.

Casually, he raised a hand and flicked the creature across the room. It struck a nearby wall and fell to the ground.

Liam watched it fade slowly from existence.

He had felt it. He had felt the turmoil in Hayley's mind, sensed it taking shape . . . he had tasted that rush of energy as she had hurled her fear at Willoughby!

Her talent – he could have reached out and touched it, embraced it.

He could have made her strong.

'You should never have been a Senior,' said Willoughby to Hayley. 'You really were never good enough.' He dismissed her from his attention, unworthy, and turned his look on Liam.

Liam shook his head, showing a confidence he wished he felt. 'No,' he said. 'Not so quick. Hayley, do it again.'

She looked at him, puzzled, and then at Willoughby.

Liam narrowed his eyes and allowed a part of his mind to open up to all the thought-shapes surging round the room. Anger, rage, *fear*. It was all so clear now. He remembered the sense of power he felt when he had been encouraged to do this in the psiLab. He focused until he found the seething mass of emotions in Hayley's mind. Her fears. Her rage. And they became *his*.

Hayley sensed that something was happening, he knew. She must feel her strength multiplying!

He had been right.

His father had been terrified of him, of what he might become. He had called Liam's gift *channelling*. They had always been careful to keep Liam's implant locked down, only opening it up to free his powers under tightly controlled conditions. *I want you to unlock my implant*, Liam had told his father back in his room. *I want you to trust me to use my talent. I want control. All this time they've been restraining me. Release me! Let me be what I am.*

Until this moment, when he tried to seize and direct Hayley's fears, he had not been sure. He had not known whether his father had really done as Liam asked, or if he had merely humoured him.

But now he knew.

Another spider materialized, this time on Willoughby's shoulder. He reached to brush it away but, before he could do so, another appeared on the back of his hand. He looked at it.

He knew something was different this time. Something was wrong.

He shook the spider off the back of his hand just as two more appeared on his jacket.

At his side, Liam could sense Hayley's confidence growing as she pushed her new strength to the limit. He could feel it in the shapes of her thoughts as she hurled her fear and her anger at Willoughby. He felt it all being channelled through him and it felt good!

More spiders appeared. On Willoughby's head and face, on his chest and arms and hands. He flicked at them and flapped at them, but there were too many.

They crawled over the principal's body and face, and Liam saw red marks where they had bitten their host.

Willoughby cried out and staggered back against the wall.

Behind him, Mr Smith stepped clear, staring wide-eyed at what was happening.

Willoughby slid to the floor, clawing at his face, scratching and scraping at the layer of spiders smothering him. Trails of blood indicated the tracks of his scratching, tearing fingernails across his own skin. He had stopped crying out now and only made strained sobbing, gasping sounds as he struggled.

It was becoming hard to see the man beneath the heaving layers of spiders.

Desperately, Willoughby crawled out through the door, trying to flee.

'Luc! Down here, now,' Liam commanded. 'You: into the room!'

Mr Smith obeyed him instantly, stepping clear of Willoughby, sidling round the wall away from Hayley.

Luc dropped into the room, bringing the rope with him, so that there was no way back up into the roof space. Liam took Hayley's arm and led her out into the corridor, where Willoughby was still crawling away under his blanket of spiders. Luc followed closely, pulling the door shut and testing to make sure it had locked itself.

Luc pointed. 'This is the way,' he said.

He was pointing the wrong way, Liam was sure.

Luc shook his head. 'We go that way and there will be more of his people there; they will stop us. *This* way, and we go down the fire escape.'

Liam nodded. It made sense now.

They ran along the corridor until they reached the end: a heavy wooden door with a metal bar across it.

'FIRE EXIT. THIS DOOR IS ALARMED.'

Luc shrugged. 'That is okay, I think. A little chaos may be our friend, no?'

He pushed at the bar and, as the door swung open, fire bells rang out through the school.

'I thought we might be needing it again!' said Luc as he dragged branches away from the car he had hidden in the trees. 'So I hid it. It was a good move, no?'

Liam grabbed a big pine branch and pulled it clear of the front of the car. They were in a stand of pine and gorse a short distance behind the school building.

Hayley cleared more branches away, eyeing them carefully for bugs before touching anything. She seemed to be full of energy, on a high after her triumph over Willoughby. 'Come on,' she said. 'Let's hit the road! I hope one of you guys can drive.'

Luc swung open a door and jumped in.

Then he climbed out and went round to the driver's side. 'You English,' he muttered as Liam and Hayley laughed. 'Always on the wrong side . . .'

Hayley jumped into the back and Liam took the front passenger seat, just as Luc fired the engine.

They accelerated forward and then Luc pulled the handbrake on and wrenched the wheel to the right, executing a perfect handbrake turn. He smiled at Liam and Hayley, who were fastening their seat belts in a hurry. He had clearly been practising.

They drove over a stretch of rough ground, then joined a track that led to the car park at the side of the main NATS building.

'The chaos,' said Luc, nodding ahead. 'Maybe not such a friend, after all . . .'

Groups of pupils milled about on the gravelled track that led round from the car park to the front of the house. Others sat on the grass or wandered aimlessly around.

Luc slowed, driving through the melee at little more than walking pace.

Liam studied the crowd, fearing that at any moment Alastair or the other Mr Smith or one of the security people would emerge and try to stop them. He thought of the flashing colours: one other thing his father had been able to do was disable that security mechanism. Alastair could not stop him with that now.

They reached the semicircle of gravel before the house and turned out on to the drive.

'Okay,' muttered Luc. 'We will be okay now, I think.'

Then a white car turned in at the far end of the drive and headed towards them.

'Oh no,' said Liam. 'I know that car.' It was the one used by Alastair and the Mr Smiths.

They watched as the car turned and stopped so that it was blocking the drive.

'What now?' said Hayley. 'They've got us, haven't they? They've still got us.'

Luc had a thoughtful look on his face. 'You know,' he said, 'in the movies, where there is a roadblock and you drive right into the middle of the car that is blocking the road and – bam! – the car has been blasted aside and you are clear? You know the movies I mean?'

Luc was speeding up.

Liam sat back, gripping the edge of the seat tightly. White knuckle tightly. 'Yes?' he said tentatively.

'Well, that is just nonsense,' said Luc. 'It would never work. Both cars would be wrecked.'

Liam looked at his driver. 'So why are you still speeding up, then?' he screeched.

Luc was staring ahead, as if willpower alone would see them through.

At the last instant, Luc twitched the driving wheel.

The car swerved, and an instant later struck the front wing of the white car in a loud explosion of noise. Liam was thrown against his seat belt as the car spun, gripped, found the road again.

He looked back. The white car had been blasted to one side of the drive. They were past it.

Their own car had come to a halt.

Luc turned, smiling, to Liam and Hayley. 'No,' he said. 'Never ram them in the middle. You should always go for either end. Then, if you are lucky, you might just spin the other car aside.' He sat upright again. He indicated back along the drive to where a small group of people were walking along towards them.

'Are you two okay?' he said. 'If so, then we should resume our journey, no?'

He put the car in gear and started to accelerate. They were about halfway along the drive.

And then he slowed once more, changing down from third gear to second, then first, then neutral. He reached down and pulled the handbrake on.

'Luc? What's the matter, Luc?' demanded Liam.

Luc turned his head towards Liam, but it was clearly a struggle. He looked puzzled, scared.

'I am sorry . . .' he said. 'My arms . . . my legs . . . they are not my own any more.'

'What do you mean?'

'I . . . they do things I do not want them to do. I cannot move them. I am sorry, my friend. I think my skills may have failed us.'

Liam climbed out of the car, still shaky after the collision.

A short distance back along the drive was the small group he had spotted before, heading towards them.

One of them was Willoughby. His face was covered in blood, the skin ripped open where he had clawed at the projected spiders.

And with him was Tsuki. He had a hand on her shoulder. A caring, paternal hand.

She was concentrating.

Liam remembered the way she had controlled that Grunt, telling his muscles what to do.

He looked back at Luc, still sitting upright in the car, confused about why his own body had stopped obeying him.

Beneath his bloody mask, Willoughby was smiling. 'Did you really think you would get away from me, Connor?' he said as he came near. 'Did you think you ever stood a chance?'

23

Sensitivity

Keep chipping away and, finally, you will break free; you will find that outer layer and realize that there are no more. Only air and sunshine and the birds singing in the trees.

They stood facing each other as the crowd gathered round them. It was like a cowboy movie: the final showdown.

Willoughby wiped blood from his face with the back of his hand.

'More spiders, Connor? Is that what you're going to try? Is that the best you can do?'

Liam shook his head. He saw his father in the crowd, talking to Mr Pullinger and one of the security guards. Father and son met each other's looks and nodded. His father had been terrified of what Liam might do with his powers when they were unlocked, but he trusted him now.

Liam returned his attention to Willoughby. He was talking to Tsuki, explaining something to her. Then the girl turned and looked at Liam, narrowing her eyes and tipping her head to one side in concentration. She was smiling too. She seemed to be enjoying this.

Liam felt the tension stealing into his muscles, starting to lock him in place as Tsuki took control.

It didn't matter. She could lock his muscles, but not his mind.

He might not be one of the special ones of Lost Families legend . . . he might just be another of Sir Peter's Follies . . . but he did have a particular, and rare, talent.

He opened himself up. He could feel the shapes that came out of people's minds all around him. The hubbub of the crowd. The bitterness and resentment so many of them felt towards Willoughby and the way he treated them. Their anger and their fear.

The crowd was waiting, suspended, as if no one knew what to do. There were divisions here: Sir Peter and his mad, obsessive followers, but also . . . the undecided. Watchers. People trying to work out if now was the moment to act . . .

Liam fed the anger back at them all, directing every one of those swirling thought-shapes back into the crowd. He felt chaos swelling, ready to break out at any moment. He could guide one person's talent, but could he handle a crowd?

Alastair pushed at someone, then ran away, but a foot snaked out and tripped him. Mr Pullinger landed on Alastair's back, pinning him down in the mud. Pushing and shoving broke out and voices erupted. Liam saw his father grab one of the Mr Smiths in a necklock, as more scuffles started up between members of the crowd and even some people Liam had never seen before.

Still the grip on Liam's muscles tightened, so that he

was gasping for breath. He looked at Willoughby.

He needed to finish this before Tsuki squeezed the life out of him!

He reached out for all those angry mind–shapes again. He sensed the swirling current of energy, trying to work out how to handle it, how to stop it overwhelming him.

And then he channelled his own sensitivity, magnifying and multiplying that angry energy, over and over. Redirecting it so that it all flowed towards a single point.

He saw Willoughby's eyes open wide, then wider, his mouth sagging open as it struck him, the onslaught of all those minds channelled into his head. Hating him. Tearing him apart.

Sir Peter put his hands to his temples, trying to shut it out, but still they flooded in, multiplied again and again by Liam's talent.

Liam could feel the mad rush as he directed it all into Willoughby's mind.

And as he sensed Willoughby's extreme anguish, Liam took this too, and channelled it, multiplied it, sent it back into the principal's head. Round and round, stronger each time he relayed it.

Something would give. Something *had* to give and it could only be Willoughby.

Liam felt hands on his arms. Hayley, Luc, his father.

'It's okay, Liam,' said his father. 'It's over now. You can stop.'

Willoughby lay on the ground, breathing shallowly. His eyes were wide open, reflecting the intense blue of the summer sky. The man lived, he breathed, his body continued to exist. But he was not there.

Liam was reminded of his mother, his biological mother. She had been just like this.

'There's a place for him,' said Liam. 'There's a place already set up for people in his state.' Let him see out the rest of his days as one of Sir Peter's Follies.

It was a blur after that. He had not expected it to wear him out so much. He remembered seeing Alastair and at least one of his Mr Smiths being led away by Mr Pullinger and a security guard. Others too.

'Come on,' his father had told him. 'Time we slipped away from all this, I think. I don't want to get drawn in.'

Liam looked around, wondering just how many of the adults at NATS had, in fact, been working under cover in one role or another. 'Who are they all?' he asked.

'Police, some of them,' said his father. 'Mostly agents with Special Intelligence, the government agency that keeps our kind in our place. And then there are all the Lost Families people. They've been monitoring things – ready to act when it was decided Sir Peter had finally gone too far. They'll clear everything up between them. No need for me to stick around.'

'No? Maybe you should,' said Liam. 'You seemed to be pretty heavily involved . . .'

They locked eyes. Eventually, Liam's father shrugged and looked away. 'I'll talk to them if that's what you want. I've only ever tried to do what's right. If you believe only one thing I've told you, you should believe that.'

'You seemed happy to let me pay the price of you doing "what's right",' said Liam.

'Not happy, son,' said his father, meeting his look again. 'So, what's it to be, then?'

Liam wasn't finished yet. 'What are *you*?' he asked. 'Whose side are *you* on?'

His father smiled. 'I'm a wild card,' he said. 'There's a network of us, working from the inside to bring down people like Willoughby. Sir Peter wanted our kind to break free and I don't have a problem with that. I *do* have a problem with how he set about it, though. People like that have to be stopped.'

They walked down through the trees, Liam, his father, Hayley and Luc.

They were heading for the creek, Liam realized. He glanced back at the school building before it was lost in the trees. 'At least it's all over now,' he said softly.

'All over?' said his father. 'You think NATS is *it*? I've been working against Willoughby for years, but there are others like him. Far too many of them . . .'

When they came to the creek, there was a sleek white yacht moored there.

Liam's father stopped and faced the three friends. 'It used to be Willoughby's,' he said, gesturing towards the boat. 'Now . . . well, it's been liberated.' He grinned and continued, 'I'll take you wherever you like. Back to your family, if that's what you choose. Hayley, where's that? Somewhere down in Kent, isn't it? And Luc – Guérande, isn't it? I think it's going to take some explaining, but we'll be okay.'

'And me?'

His father looked at Liam. 'It's like I told you. You have a choice. I can't make these decisions for you.'

Liam nodded. He had plenty of time yet. All the time it would take to sail down to France to deliver Luc back to his parents.

Sometimes you just have to leap in, take the plunge. But sometimes it's better to sit back and see how things turn out.